Thomas Letchworth

Twelve Discourses

Delivered chiefly at the meeting-house of the people called Quakers, in the Park,

Southwark

Thomas Letchworth

Twelve Discourses
Delivered chiefly at the meeting-house of the people called Quakers, in the Park, Southwark

ISBN/EAN: 9783337426446

Printed in Europe, USA, Canada, Australia, Japan

Cover: Foto ©Andreas Hilbeck / pixelio.de

More available books at **www.hansebooks.com**

TWELVE
DISCOURSES,

DELIVERED CHIEFLY AT

THE MEETING-HOUSE

OF THE PEOPLE CALLED

QUAKERS,

IN THE PARK,

Southwark,

BY THE LATE

THOMAS LETCHWORTH.

———————

LONDON:

Printed by J. W. GALABIN, Ingram-Court, Fenchurch-
ftreet, for
W. RICHARDSON, at the Royal-Exchange.

M.DCC.LXXXVII.

PREFACE.

THESE Difcourfes were taken in fhort-hand at the time of delivery, by a perfon not in the fame religious community with the preacher. A few neceffary corrections of grammatical inaccuracies have been fince made ; and, in fome inftances, a more complete citation of the texts adduced. In quotations made from memory, it muft frequently happen that the words are not quite exact. It fuf-

ficiently

ficiently anfwered the fpeaker's purpofe if the general import of the paffage was conveyed, and expreffions, which thus qualify the citation, are frequently introduced, and always to be implied.

It is well known that the minifters of the religious fociety, with whom the author of thefe Difcourfes profeffed, difclaim all previous ftudy in the compofition of their extemporaneous fermons. It cannot, therefore, be expected that they fhould be exact in methodical arrangement, or abound in the embellifhments of modern eloquence. What was not attempted it is no difgrace not to have attained. It may, however, perhaps, juftly be a matter of doubt whether that zeal and energy of delivery, which arife from the feelings of the moment, may not, in their effects on the audience, more than counterbalance the cool correctnefs of ftudied oratory. The Quakers lay down few dogmas, and feldom enlarge on thofe myfterious points of theology which have fo much divided the Chriftian world, and

have

have moftly occafioned contention in proportion to their obfcurity. The doctrine
of univerfal grace, of which a manifeftation, or portion, is given to every man,
and by obedience to which he is enabled to
fulfil his duty, and to walk acceptably with
his Creator, is the leading principle of that
fociety, who hold, as the neceffary refult
of it, that true worfhip confifts in a humble proftration of heart and communion of
fpirit with the Father of mercies, and is
therefore perfectly confiftent with a ftate
of filence. Thefe points are inculcated in
the following pages, perhaps, to a degree of
tautology, for which an extract from one
of the Difcourfes, in the preacher's own
words, may furnifh the beft excufe.

" Though it is probable that what I
" have fometimes delivered may have been
" more or lefs fimilar to that which I have
" aforetime delivered, yet I hope that even
" a repetition of doctrines and advices,
" which we are urged to deliver from a
" fenfe of duty, may not be as water fpilt

" upon

" upon a ſtone, but may have a tendency
" (if not to convey any material informa-
" tion to the underſtanding) to ſtir up at
" leaſt the pure mind by way of remem-
" brance."

The love of fame, taken as a general
principle, and including the deſire of being
eſteemed and approved by one's friends,
frequently mingles itſelf with our beſt motives. But, though this paſſion may, in a
public preacher, receive ſome gratification
from the ſilent and ſolemn attention of the
hearers, it would ſcarcely excite a prudent
man to expect any increaſe of reputation
from the publication of Diſcourſes, of
which the ſubject and arrangement were
not pre-conceived, and the expreſſions ſuch
as were ſuggeſted at the inſtant. In the
preſent inſtance, at leaſt, no imputation of
this ſort can ariſe to the author of theſe
Diſcourſes, who is removed from the ſcene;
and the influence of all earthly paſſions.
The apology for the preſent publication
reſts on the hope that impreſſions of a ſalu-
tary

tary nature may, by this means, be renewed on fuch minds as are fincerely defirous
of fulfilling the duties of their ftation, and
of reaching the haven of eternal reft.

A friend of the author has favoured us
with the following brief account of him.

Thomas Letchworth was born at Wood-
bridge, in the county of Suffolk, in the
year 1739. His parents were of the people
called Quakers, and his father, a tradef-
man in that town, was a preacher among
them. In that religious fociety, the earn-
ings of honeft induftry are thought to be a
mode of maintenance more confiftent with
the evangelical qualifications required in a
Chriftian minifter, and with the influence
he ought to poffefs in his congregation,
than legal ftipends or gratuitous contribu-
tions, which too frequently occafion contention in the one inftance, or dependence
in the other. He received from his father,
who had a numerous family, the common
education of a boarding-fchool at Hart-
ford, and was afterwards put apprentice to

a linen-draper at Epping. In the early part of his life, he was of a confumptive habit ; and this imperfect ftate of his health probably confpired with a difpofition, naturally reflective and ferious, to imprefs on his mind a ftrong fenfe of the vanity of human defires, and the importance of religious duty. Before he was twenty years of age, he began his minifterial fervices, in which he was particularly defirous to inculcate on the minds of young people a frequent confideration of their latter end, and of the awful concerns of futurity. His Difcourfes were copious, animated, and pathetic ; but, perhaps, not altogether free from a certain inflation of language, to which men of fervid imaginations, in expreffing their firft conceptions, are frequently fubject. His fervices were, however, moftly acceptable, and he fpent a confiderable portion of his time in vifiting different parts of the country on a religious account. At t is period, he kept a fhop in Crifpin-ftreet, Spital-fields, whence he removed to

Ampthill,

Ampthill, in Bedfordſhire, but afterwards returned to London, in which city, or its vicinity, he continued to reſide till near his deceaſe.

He was not much converſant in the learn-ed languages, but his reading in his native tongue was pretty extenſive. Hiſtory, natural philoſophy, the rudiments of medicine and anatomy, the leading principles of aſtronomy, and even the charms of poetry, furniſhed him with matter of meditation and amuſement in his leiſure hours. But his favourite ſtudy was the myſterious operations of the human mind, the paſſions which actuate it, the nature of its union with the body, the reaſonable hope of its immortality, the principles of identity, liberty, neceſſity, and all thoſe branches which conſtitute the ſublime but obſcure ſcience of metaphyſics. He was well verſed in moſt of the writers on theſe ſubjects, nor did the different opinions of religious ſects, both in his own and in former periods of hiſtory, eſcape his cloſe examination. The *dernier reſult* of his en-

quiries

quiries may be learned from the following paper, found among his manuscripts with that very title ; and it were to be wished that every inquiry and controversy concerning such subjects might terminate in the same humble and liberal manner.

" From an honest intention of acting
" consistently with the relation I bear to
" God, my Maker, and to my fellow-crea-
" tures, I have carefully reviewed most of
" the religious sentiments, on those subjects,
" held by any society of men in the known
" world. I have put a period to my re-
" searches into the books and opinions of
" men, and have concluded to resign my-
" self in future to the guidance of those
" sensations which I feel to increase my
" love to God and to mankind, and to pur-
" sue such measures of conduct in religion
" and morality, the prosecution of which
" gives me the most peace ; and to judge no
" man, neither pretend to exalt my opinions
" and practices to judge of the rectitude of o-
" ther mens by. Let others do as they
. " will,

" will, as for me I will endeavour to feek
" peace, and enfue it. A man cannot be
" happy, whatever notions, or opinions,
" he may hold, or whatever meafures of
" conduct he may purfue, unlefs, in the
" holding of fuch opinions, and in being
" found in the profecution of fuch mea-
" fures, he feels himfelf eafy and comfort-
" ed at heart. Let this rule of my future
" conduct be termed erroneous, defective,
" an illufion, or what not — it is the beft
" rule of my faith and manners which I
" have been able to find after a clofe enqui-
" ry of fifteen years. *Glory to God in the
" higheft, on earth peace, and good-will to
" men,* is, and I hope ever will be, the lan-
" guage of my foul. Amen."

At what time this fummary of his re-
fearches was written does not appear; probably fome years before his deceafe. The
following extracts from three letters, written
to a friend during his laft illnefs, the two latter a fhort time before his death, will fhew
that thefe fentiments retained their impreffion

fion to the laft: they will fhew that he poffeffed what, in fuch moments, it is better to poffefs than the treafures of the rich or the knowledge of the learned, a fpirit of refignation and peace, and a humble but earneft hope in the mercies of the Almighty.

" *Fourteenth of the twelfth month*, 1783. I
" am now better than when thou lefteft me.
" My little bark fprang a leak fome months
" ago, which gradually gained on the pump
" until every effort to fave her feemed to be
" made in vain, and deftruction feemed in-
" evitable. The moment was awful, but
" not fearful. I felt an entire refignation
" to the appointment of our heavenly Fa-
" ther. I have not to tell of being lifted
" up to extacy in vifions, nor of my fears
" having been alarmed by any terrific
" dreams. To God, my Maker, I looked
" fingly. My dependence was fixed on
" him alone. A fober humbling fenfe of
" his prefence and providence prevented
" fear, and infpired hope."

" *Eleventh*

" *Eleventh of the ninth month,* 1784. I
" find myself still losing flesh, and rather
" weaker, but, in some other respects, ra-
" ther better. I know not what to think.
" Here I am.

> " Safe in the hands of one disposing Power,
> " Or in the natal, or the mortal, hour,"

" enjoying every gleam of sunshine to
" the utmost, and bearing, with as much
" patience and resignation as possible, the
" cloudy days and starless nights some-
" times allotted me under the present dif-
" pensation."

" *Twenty-eighth of the tenth month*, 1784.
" This disorder has much reduced my flesh
" and my strength; but I am scarcely in
" any pain; nor am I sensible at present of
" any symptom which threatens any. The
" account I received by thy letter of our
" friend ****** affected me much. We
" seem to be in a similar weak state, and
" as it were dissolving apace into the earth
" whence we originally sprang; for, *as*
" *thou art, and to dust thou shalt return:*
" and, whenever we die, whether soon or
" late,

" late, I hope we fhall have an unfhaken
" truft in the common Father of us all,
" and refign to the common lot of all flefh
" with compofure and without regret. Re-
" member me not as a forfaken and mifera-
" ble man, for I enjoy even now, and fuf-
" fer but little, very little, comparatively
" fpeaking. I rejoice in the good provi-
" dence of God, which is over us all con-
" tinually for our good, and is alike gra-
" cious to all his creatures in what he gives
" and what he denies them. And, in all
" the difpenfations of his wifdom, let us
" truft in him, our common Father, Pro-
" tector, and Friend."

He at length gradually funk under the
flow but irrefiftible force of a confumption,
and departed on the 7th of the eleventh
month, (November,) 1784, at the houfe of
a friend at Newbury, in Berkfhire. From
the foregoing account of the ftate of his
mind, it is almoft needlefs to add that he
met death with a becoming and humble fortitude. He was interred, at his own re-
quest,

queſt, in the Quakers burial-ground at Reading, on the 14th of the month above-mentioned; and his funeral was attended by a great number of his friends, who were deſirous of teſtifying their eſteem for his memory by this laſt mark of attention.

N. B. *The firſt Diſcourſe in this collection has been incorrectly printed in Ireland, and attributed to another preacher. It is now printed from a more correct copy, and reſtored to the proper owner.*

DISCOURSE

DISCOURSES.

DISCOURSE I.

THERE is a paſſage of ſacred writ which has been revived in my remembrance during the ſilence of this meeting; and the train of reflections which it excited has ſealed inſtruction to my mind, and furniſhed me with renewed cauſe for humiliation and gratitude. The import of it is this : *Men and brethren, what ſhall we do to be ſaved?*

No perſon, who ſeriouſly believes in the exiſtence of a God, in a future ſtate, and in the awful doctrine of rewards and pu-

B   niſhments,

nifhments, can be indifferent refpecting what may be his lot, when he fhall be dif-poffeffed of this frail tabernacle of clay which he now inhabits, and which is ap-proaching to the period of its diffolution. It cannot be a matter of indifference to him, whether he fhall finally receive the ir-revocable fentence of *Go, ye curfed,* into the regions of unfpeakable mifery; or, *Come, ye bleffed of my Father,* inherit the kingdom prepared for the righteous ;— en-ter thou into the joy of thy Lord, and into thy Mafter's reft.

This concern has prompted many to en-quire what is effentially neceffary for them to believe and practife, in order to render themfelves the proper objects of divine complacence, and furnifh them with a well-grounded hope of a happy and glo-rious immortality.

The honeft and fincere, in every nation under heaven, have formed different ideas of the requifites of falvation; and they have, of courfe, purfued as different mea-fures

fures to accomplifh that defirable and bleffed end.

It does not appear to be my prefent bufinefs to particuiarife any of the various
fyftems of faith which are adopted by any
party amongft mankind. It is not to con-
trovert matters in which fincere men of various denominations moft furely believe,
but rather to recommend them to ftand o-
pen always to conviction, and to a ftrict
attention to thofe rules of conduct, which,
on an impartial examination, appear to
them moft agreeable to the will of heaven.
I fhall therefore addrefs myfelf to thofe, in
whatever religious fociety they are found,
whofe honeft inquiries have not yet been
attended with fufficient conviction, — have
not yet led them clearly to perceive what
the terms are on which their future happi-
pinefs depends, and are, therefore, looking
one upon another, whilft this important
queftion is found at leaft in their *hearts*,
if not in their *mouths, Men and brethren,
what fhall we do to be faved ?* An inquiry of

this

this folemn nature, arifing from a proper fenfibility of the want of better inftruction, is an indication of that concern and holy anxiety which will ever be acceptable to the Father of fure mercies. He regards fuch humble inquirers, after truth and peace with him, with gracious condefcenfion, and, if they rely on the guidance of his Spirit, will finally conduct them to his glorious reft.

I fhall not prefume arrogantly to dictate to any, refpecting matters of fo important a concern as that of the foul's falvation. Every man fhould exercife thofe talents and gifts, with which the Father of Lights has endued him, in a clofe and fincere attention to the voice of the internal teacher, and in the difcovery of thofe truths, both practical and fpeculative, which have an immediate relation to the happinefs of a being circumftanced as he is. I fhall fimply propofe thofe things which, in my view, and from my own experience as an individual, appear

pear to me worthy of God for their author, and worthy of man's moſt ſerious attention.

It is an indiſputable truth that we made not ourſelves : *It is he that hath made us,* ſaid the Pſalmiſt, *and not we ourſelves,* for *we are alſo his offspring.* The matter which forms the univerſe, the vehicles which the ſoul informs, and the more noble intellectual powers and faculties we poſſeſs, derive their being from the eternal Fountain of all power and intelligence, whom we characteriſe by the awful names of Jah, Jehovah, and God. It is alſo indiſputably evident to me, that we were brought into exiſtence with the benevolent deſign of our finally ſuſtaining the confluent dignities of glory, honour, immortality, and eternal life. The Lord Almighty hath, in unſpeakable mercy, deſigned, that, after we have endured a ſeaſon of probation, a conflict with our paſſions, excited by numerous cauſes, and a fight of afflictions, we ſhould finally receive a glorious reward, a

perpetuity

perpetuity of unmixed felicity, in the regions of eternity.

But this defirable and excellent end is not to be effected by what is generally called Fate, the laws of neceffity, or the arbitrary will, power, or decree, of the Author of our exiftence. God hath, in his wifdom, conftituted. us free and intelligent beings. He has endued us with faculties and powers capable of apprehending and practifing thofe effential duties which he makes the condition of our final acceptance with him. He offers, but does not impofe ; he gracioufly invites, but does not compel, us to accept of happinefs. He fhews us the fpiritual Canaan, the land of the faints inheritance, in every generation : he gives us power to poffefs, but does not compel us to enter therein. Good and evil are clearly fet before us, but our election is not conftrained to either. The oeconomy of his moral government over rational beings is laid in divine wifdom and eternal righteoufnefs. The great Sovereign of the univerfe

is

is no refpecter of perfons; for, of one
blood hath he made all nations that dwell
on the face of the earth. They ftand in
the fame relation to the univerfal Father,
Shepherd, and Bifhop, of fouls, who ten-
derly invites the whole race of mankind to
come unto him that they may finally inherit
the joy of his falvation. O unfpeakable mercy ! unutterable theme ! It is fufficient to
awaken the moft glowing fenfations of exalted and grateful praife to that God who is
the falvation and glory of the righteous generations, *the rock of their ftrength, and their
everlafting refuge.*

To this doctrine the holy apoftle bore an
ample and explicit teftimony : *Of a truth,*
(faid he,) *I perceive that God is no refpecter
of perfons, but, in every nation, he that feareth him, and worketh righteoufnefs, is accepted
with him.*

Thus we find that it is the fear of the
Lord, and an obedience to the law of righteoufnefs, which are the terms alone by

B 4   which

which men can be faved. *If ye live after the flefh, ye fhall die ; but, if ye, through the fpirit, mortify the deeds of the body, ye fhall live.* This is a propofition of univerfal importance ; a propofition which relates to every individual in the vaft community of mankind, however circumftanced, whether bond or free, rich or poor, or in whatever climate they refide.

All this may, indeed, be acknowledged both by thofe within and without the audience of my voice, who yet are in doubt *what they fhall do to be faved* with an everlafting falvation. They want to be informed of the precife ideas that fhould be affixed to the conditions contained in the text ; although, perhaps, they readily apprehend that the terms *life* and *death* mean future happinefs and mifery.

I fhall therefore attempt, according to the ability I am endued with at this feafon, to give you my thoughts on the important fubject under confideration.

To

To live after the flesh is to live in the gratification of our animal appetites and paffions beyond the bounds of reafon, temperance, and fobriety. All the works of
darknefs, which, by the fame apoftle, are
termed *deeds of the body*, all pride, wrath,
envy, hatred, covetoufnefs, with all the de-
ceivablenefs of unrighteoufnefs, are, in o-
ther words, *living after the flesh*. Thefe
things not only tend to the injury of peace
and fociety, and are a bane to that happinefs which is the refult of genuine virtue e-
ven in this life ; not only introduce numerous errors into the animal and moral fyftem, and aggravate the infirmities to which
thefe bodies are incident, but render us unfit for thofe contemplations, and that fupreme felicity, which are adapted to the
dignity of rational and immortal fpirits.
God, in his wifdom, hath made man a little (and perhaps but a little) lower than
the angels. He has endued him with a capacity for contemplating and adoring him,
the fource of uncreated excellence and perfection,

fection, and would crown him with fuperior honour, glory, and happinefs, to what
fenfual gratifications can ever afford. Let
us not then degrade ourfelves beneath that
rank we were defigned to fill in creation,
but remember our immortal defcent, the
caufe of our being, and its end.

We have, indeed, bodies, and are impri-
foned within elements, which excite within
us numerous appetites, affections, and paffions; but all thefe are to be gratified within certain bounds, in a degree proportion-
ed to our exigences and neceffities, of which
the fupreme intelligence has implanted
a principle within us to judge.

This principle of intelligence, although
called by a variety of names, and diftinguifhed by various appellations, in the various profeffions amongft men, is one in
nature, and univerfal amongft mankind.
It is the fpirit in man that giveth a right
underftanding : it is the light that (more
or lefs) enlightens every man: it is the
word of God in the heart, and the word of
faith

faith which the apoftle preached to the Gentiles : it is the grace that hath appeared unto all men, teaching them to deny all ungodlinefs and the world's lufts, and to live
righteoufly, foberly, and godly, in this prefent world : and, finally, it is the fupreme
reafon, the law of truth and rectitude, the
teft of virtue and vice, which God himfelf
hath placed in the hearts of all men; and
happy are thofe who hear and obey it in all
things.

I would not be underftood to mean that
this principle, of which I am fpeaking, is
defigned to inftruct us in all truths which
the human mind may, in its own activity
and wifdom, attempt to inveftigate ; or to
give us a clear infight into thofe numerous
fpeculative fubjects, which have not only
unprofitably employed mankind, and di-
verted their attention from things more
fubftantial, but which have perplexed and
divided them from generation to generation.

But,

But, by the exercife of this pure, holy, heavenly, principle, we may apprehend thofe truths which belong to us, and which have an effential relation to the prime end of our being. Of thefe truths the Father of Spirits has conftituted man an adequate judge.

This is implied by the queftion which our Lord himfelf propofed to a people mifled by the traditions of their fathers, and who had, through the neglect of this principle, taken for doctrine the commandments of men : *Yea, and why, even of yourfelves, judge ye not what is right ?*

The obligation to all our focial, relative, and religious, duties arifes from the rela-tions we ftand in to our fellow-creatures and to God, the holy author of our exiftence. The general relation, which our fellow-crea-tures ftand in to us, is that of brethren, children of the fame univerfal parent, fub-ject to the fame neceffities, and formed for the fame unfpeakably glorious and happy end. Hence it is our duty to exercife the

amiable

amiable virtues of love, forbearance, kindnefs, and charity, to all around us ; to feek their happinefs, and lighten the weight of human mifery to the utmoft of our power.

There are, alfo, various accidental relations amongft mankind, as mafter, fervant, father, governor, and numerous others ; all which have their correfpondent duties.

The relation we ftand in to the great Author of our being is that of children, which is one and immutable at all times. A life, agreeable to that relation we ftand in to the Lord Almighty, is that of filial fear. Obedience and worfhip are our indifpenfable duty to him ; and the rules of juftice, charity, and brotherly kindnefs, are indifpenfable obligations on us to the reft of mankind.

Thus far, perhaps, the perfons, whom I immediately addrefs at this time, may concur with me in fentiment : but they, as well as myfelf, are perhaps confcious of having failed in numerous inftances of dif-

charging

charging their religious duties to God, and their focial duties one to another.

We have all finned, and fallen fhort of the glory of God. We have multiplied our tranf-greffions without number, and our mani-fold iniquities rife before us as a thick cloud, obfcuring the brightnefs of that Sun of eternal Righteoufnefs, which would o-therwife illuminate our underftandings with its marvellous lights. *Who, therefore,* (fays the humiliated penitent foul,) *fhall deliver us from the body of this death ?* Who fhall take from us the weight of our fins, under which we groan inceffantly ? *Who fhall de-liver us from the wrath to come ? Men and brethren, what fhall we do to be faved ?*

The conditions of our redemption, and reconciliation with the gracious Father of us all, are clearly expreffed in the oracles of facred truth. The placability of the di-vine nature is repeatedly afferted. He, with whom dwells wifdom, juftice, righteouf-nefs, and ftrength, is alfo reprefented to us in the glorious adorable character of a God

of

of mercy, long-fuffering, and never-failing kindnefs; as a Being ready to blot out our tranfgreffions from the celeftial regifter on our fincere repentance, and to remember them no more. He will reftore unto the humble penitent the joy of his falvation: he will guide him by his counfel, and afterwards receive him into glory.

This important and interefting doctrine was typified under the law, fpoken of by the prophets, and glorioufly afferted by the Son of God, who is our mediator with the Father, and the hope of all the righteous generations. In his character was difplayed to mankind, in the moft eminent and ftriking manner, the provident care, mercy, and goodnefs, of God towards his whole rational creation. Like fheep they have gone aftray from the univerfal Shepherd and Bifhop of fouls. They have revolted from his government, and widely wandered from the path of purity and holinefs, which is alfo the path of pleafantnefs and peace; that path of moral rectitude and truth, that

bright

bright and shining light, which (like the luminous orb after it arises in our hemisphere) shines with increasing refulgence and splendor till it arrive at the meridian altitude of glorious perfect day. The light, which shines from heaven on the understandings of men, will lead all those, who pursue its direction, by degrees of experience, through the wilderness of this world in perfect safety : it will bring them, when the days of their warfare are accomplished, to the grand end of their creation, — to that complete fruition of bliss, which is figuratively represented to us by a city that has foundations, whose builder and maker is God ; a city, whose walls are salvation, and whose gates are eternal praise ; a city, that has no need of the elementary light of the sun, moon, or stars ; for, the Lord God and the Lamb are the light thereof : a city, where God reigneth triumphantly amongst his saints, and is to them an inexhaustible fountain of joy, light, and felicity, for ever. There the weary tribula-

ted

ted pilgrim finds an end of all his anxiety and labour ; the days of his mourning are ended, and he receives the reward of his faith and patience, the fruition of his hopes, even the eternal falvation of his foul.

The important meffage which Chrift, the glorious high-prieft of the Chriftian religion, had in commiffion from his and our Father, from his and our God, was, that he compaffionated his creatures, incompaffed with the diftreffes that their fins had brought upon them, — that he willed not their everlafting feparation from him, the fource of happinefs, but that he was willing they fhould be reconciled to him. For this end, he called upon them to *repent and be converted*, that their fins might be forgiven them, and that they might finally enter into his reft.

This was the interefting doctrine which the Saviour of the world promulgated, and happy are thofe who hear and obey it !

Repent, and be converted, that your fins may be forgiven you. It is not the affent of the

lip,

lip, and of the tongue, to the glorious truths of the gospel; it is not the splendid formality of high profession; it is not crying Lord, Lord! in the hour of strong conviction; but it is a surrender of the will and affections, a renovation of the heart and conformity to the divine image, which can alone gain us an admittance into the New Jerusalem, the city of God.

If we make an impartial survey of our past lives, review our frequent revoltings, and compare our conduct with the convictions we have received of right and wrong, virtue and vice, there is scarcely a soul present but must feel some degree of remorse, some degree of repentance, for the turpitude of his morals, and his want of love, obedience, and gratitude, to so gracious a Father, who has encompassed us with blessings, and preserved us, by his providence, from the earliest period of our lives to the present hour. On these solemn reflections we must (I say again) witness some degree of repentance;

repentance ; but, unhappily for us, the im-
preffions that are made on our minds, on a
ferious review of our actions, are foon cancelled, foon effaced, by the influence which
a variety of creaturely objects are fuffered
to make upon us, and, like the early dew,
they foon pafs away : *Of the rock that begat*
them they have been unmindful. Cleanfed, in
fome degree, as we are by the waters of
contrition, we again become defiled by a
repetition of that iniquity, which, in the
moments of our humiliation, we had determined to renounce and forfake. We are a-
gain caught in the fnare of our lufts, and
captivated by objects which have a tendency to alienate our affections from the one
adorable Object, the fource of our fafety and
felicity, the only permanent and fupreme
good. What is to be done in the fatal di-
lemma to which our inconftancy to our
virtuous refolutions has reduced us ? Shall
we defpair of the divine mercy, which we
have fo often abufed ; of that goodnefs we
have fo long trifled with ? or, fear that our

future

future endeavours will be vain, and that, for our multiplied tranfgreffions, we fhall be made *a defolation for ever !* God forbid ! Let us rather, in the depths of felf-abafe-ment, proftrate our fouls at the throne of grace, and humbly implore the continued mercy of the univerfal Parent. Let us beg for ftrength and holy ability to withftand fucceeding temptations, and run the ways of his commandments with delight.

As a father pitieth his children, fo he pitieth thofe who fear him, and, in immor-tal kindnefs, will bring them to the joy of his falvation. He knoweth our frame, and remembereth that we are but duft. Al-though he hideth his face for a moment, yet with everlafting kindnefs will he remember Zion ; for, *her maker is her hufband, the Lord of Hofts is his name.* Let us there-fore befeech him, in the fervency of pray-er,. to fend forth help from his holy fanctu-ary, and ftrengthen us to renew and keep our covenants with him to the end of our days.

Let

Let us refrain from the commiffion of evil, and wait on him in the filence of all flefh, that the Fountain of light and truth may again enlighten us to fee ourfelves as we are feen of him, and inflame our hearts with that celeftial fire which purgeth away the intellectual filth and drofs that prevent the afcent of the foul God-ward, and render it an unfit habitation for his holinefs to dwell in. As our own backflidings have frequently corrected us, and covered our minds with anxiety, let our future conduct, directed by his grace, atone for what is paft, and, by a converfation ordered aright, let us *glorify our Father who is in heaven.*

I feel, at this feafon, the influence (in degree) of that celeftial charity which breathes through Immanuel to the whole creation of God, and wifheth falvation to every foul that inhabits the earth. In that I intreat you, as a being fubject to the fame infirmities which you fometimes unavailably deplore, *Repent, and be converted.* Repentance you have frequently experienced, but

too

too little, I fear, of that effential converfion which the gofpel of Jefus propofes.
It is highly probable that fome perfons prefent have feen the neceffity of that renovation of heart, and reformation of manners,
intended by converfion ; and yet, urged by
the powerful prevalence of their lufts and
of felf-love, are feeking, if poffible, to find
fome other remedy for a wounded confcience than that which the fimplicity of the
gofpel requires as a neceffary prelude to the
favour of God. They are enquiring *What
fhall we do to be faved ?* and, like the young
man in the gofpel, they have been animated
with a defire to be inrolled among the difciples of Jefus, who are called heirs of
God, and co-heirs with Chrift, of that inheritance which is incorruptible and full of
glory. They have afked counfel of the
wonderful Counfellor, and addreffed him
with the important queftion, *What good
thing fhall I do that I may inherit eternal life?*
yet, when the unchangeable terms of falvation have been propofed ; when they have

been

been told they muſt part with all their i-
dols, they have gone away ſorrowful : the
terms have appeared too hard for them to
comply with ; and, like the king who
wanted to be cured of his leproſy, and was
ſtaggered at the thought of taking ſo long a
journey as the prophet had directed, are
crying out, *Are not Abana and Pharphar,
rivers of Damaſcus, better than all the waters
of Iſrael ?* will not their waters cleanſe
me from my impurity ?

Thus, numbers among mankind are
ſtriving to elude thoſe meaſures which the
goſpel of Jeſus enjoins, and are ſubſtituting
others in their ſtead, which are better a-
dapted to ſoothe the carnal mind, and prevent that mortification of the deeds of the
body which human nature ſhrinks from
with horror. Man is deſirous to poſſeſs the
crown of eternal life, but not willing to
bear the croſs. He would indeed reign with
Chriſt, but not ſuffer with him. He would
accompany him to the mount of transfigu-
ration, but not to Golgotha. He would be

his

his attendant at his glorification, but not in the awful fcenes of his humiliation.

Divers have wandered as from mountain to mountain and from hill to hill, feeking for the living in the fepulchres of the dead. They have fometimes adopted one creed, and fometimes another,—practifed external ordinances, and complied with empty forms; addreffing themfelves frequently to guides, as blind and impotent as themfelves, with this awful query, *Men and brethren, what fhall we do to be faved?*

I fay again, repent, and be converted; for, this is the only way to find falvation to your fouls. No external ceremonies, no verbal confeffions, no change of opinions merely, can accomplifh this repentance and converfion, and afford you the confequent rewards of a glorious immortality. This important work of falvation cannot be effected in man's time, will, activity, or wifdom, but is wrought in him by the powerful operation of the Holy Ghoft, which is as a confuming fire to the adverfa-

ry,

ry, to the adverfe part of man, to the corrupt will, which would not that Chrift
fhould reign in his kingdom, and that
God fhould be all in all.

It is the baptifm of fire, of which John's
was but a type, which, difcriminating the
pure from the impure, gathers the wheat
into the garner, but confumes the chaff
with unquenchable burnings.

In the world there are many voices
which correfpond not with the voice of
Chrift, the only Shepherd and Bifhop of
fouls, whom we ought to hear and obey in
all things, but which are the voices of thofe
who *teach for hire, and divine for money:
who look for their gain from their quarters,*
and are ready to make war againft confcien-
tious men, who cannot put into their
mouths. Thefe have found it their worldly intereft to lead the deluded people from,
rather than to, Chrift, the glorious high-
prieft, the life and light of men. They
have attempted to render that myfterious
which the Holy Ghoft has left clear, and to

perplex

perplex the underftandings of men with vain metaphyfical fpeculations, without making them either wifer or better. This clafs of men, whofe *God is their belly, whofe glory is their fhame,* have indeed proved *phyficians of no value.*

Many have enquired of thefe, *What fhall we do to be faved?* but they, not having experienced the work of falvation in themfelves, are incapable to inftruct others in the way that leads to eternal life. Inftead of laying the axe to the root of the corrupt tree, they have only attempted to lop off fome of its branches, and refcind fome of its moft palpable excrefcences. They have been crying, Peace, peace! when the alarm of danger fhould have founded in the ears of the people. They have prefcribed emollients where the moft fearching operation was expedient ; and, healing the wound of the daughter of Zion deceitfully, have lulled multitudes into a fatal fecurity, by flattering them with hopes, which, it is to

be

be feared, will end in confufion and difappointment, and perifh for ever.

There are others who affume the office
of minifters, the purity of whofe inten-
tions charity forbids me to difpute; who,
like a man that attempts to anfwer a queftion before he has fully heard it, have too
precipitately embarked in the important
work of inftructing fouls in the great things
of falvation. Thefe are, like Ephraim,
a cake not turned ; are not yet inftructed in
the way of the Lord perfectly, and, whilft
they are teaching others, had need themfelves to be taught what are the firft principles of the oracles of God. The coal
from the holy altar has not yet been applied to their lips, and they have been mi-
niftering, by the law of a carnal commandment, without being endued with the power of an endlefs life. They have run on
the Lord's errand unfent, and have not effentially profited the people. They have
taken upon them to guide thofe who are inquiring *what fhall we do to be faved,* and have
led

led them indeed from the confines of Egypt, but leave them, undirected to the fpiritual Mofes, to wander in uncertainty, and to compafs a mountain of doubts in the wildernefs.

May the Lord Almighty, in his infinite mercy, gather thefe who are wandering as fheep without a fhepherd, and lead them into the facred inclofures of his fold of eternal reft and fafety !

May the nations of them that have fat in darknefs be again enlightened by the glorious breaking forth of the Sun of righteoufnefs in their hearts, that our Zion may yet become an eternal excellency, and the joy of many generations !

Let it not be thought, by any thing I have faid, that I look upon all, who appear girded with the linen ephod of other Chriftian focieties, either as impoftors, or the deluded votaries of Antichrift. I freely declare I doubt not but many of them have had a difpenfation of the gofpel committed to them ; and, although they may be bi-
affed

affed by the prejudice of education and the
traditions of their fathers, yet the root of
the matter feems to be in them. I efteem
thefe, in whatever fociety they are found,
and in whatever veftments they are clothed,
as my brethren in the fellowfhip of the e-
verlafting gofpel of Chrift. Yet I cannot
direct the fearcher after truth, who is pen-
fively inquiring *What he fhall do to be faved,*
to the miniftry of any man ; but would rather recommend him to the immediate
teaching of the word nigh in the heart, e-
ven the fpirit of God. This is the only infallible teacher, and the primary adequate
rule of faith and, manners, and will lead
thofe who attend to its dictates into the
peaceable paths of fafety and of truth.
Let the earneft humble petition of your
·fouls be, to the Father of fure mercies,
*Lead me by thy counfel, and afterwards receive
me into glory :* let thy rod and thy ftaff fupport me, through the uncertainties of time,
to a happy conclufion in thy favour. Ye
need not, faith the apoftle to the church
formerly,

formerly, that any man teach you, save as this anointing teacheth, which is truth, and no lie. Ceafe, therefore, from man, whofe breath is in his noftrils, and whofe exiftence is but as a vapour ; for, wherein is he to be accounted of ? As a fallible being he is fubject to frequent deception, and is therefore liable to deceive ; but the fpirit of God can neither be deceived, nor will it deceive any foul that fubmits to its holy government, and obeys its dictates. In this is our fafety and ftrength, and the hope of our eternal reward, when our weary pilgrimage fhall come to an end.

O ye penitent prodigals, my foul earneftly longs for your reftoration to the mercy and favour of God !

Ye, who are reduced, by your wanderings in the wildernefs of this world, to a ftate of extreme poverty, to the want of that bread which comes down from the celeftial regions, and which can alone nourifh the foul up to eternal life ; — ye, who have long been attempting to fatisfy the cravings of an immortal

mortal fpirit with the hufks and fhells of
an empty profeffion of religion, look towards your Father, from whom you have
revolted. Remember that in his houfe there
is bread enough, and to fpare : there your
fouls may be richly replenifhed with endu-
ring fubftance. Return, O houfe of Ifrael,
from your backflidings, and feek the face
of your everlafting Father and Friend! In
unfpeakable kindnefs he hath declared that
he will be found of thofe who feek him in
finccrity of heart; and that as many as
knock at his gate for an entrance fhall be
admitted to his prefence, and receive the remiffion of their fins. O unfpeakable condefcenfion ! unutterable love ! Though
glorioufly exalted above the heaven of heavens, and placed at the fummit of all perfection, yet his gracious regard is to the
fons of men, and he is *beautifying the place
of his feet.*

The humble addrefs which the prodigal
made to his father, the return that he met
with, and the manner of his reception into
favour,

favour, are exceedingly expreſſive of the becoming penitence of the one, and the mercy and benignity of the other. *I have ſinned againſt heaven, and in thy ſight, and am no longer worthy to be called thy ſon; make me therefore as one of thy hired ſervants.* The injured neglected parent compaſſionates his diſtreſs, takes the prodigal in his arms, owns him for his ſon, orders the fatted calf to be killed, and rebukes the envy of his elder brother with *this my ſon is dead, but he is alive again; he was loſt, but is found.* O the height and depth of the goodneſs and mercy of God! Look unto him, ye ends of the earth, and be ſaved!

Before I conclude, I find it in mine heart to addreſs another claſs in this meeting: a claſs who have earneſtly ſought, and happily found, him of whom Moſes and the prophets did write, Jeſus of Nazareth, the Immanuel, which, being interpreted, is, God with us. You, who once were ſcattered as ſheep without a ſhepherd on the barren mountains and deſolate hills of an empty profeſſion, the great Shepherd

Shepherd of fouls hath gathered within the facred inclofures of his fold, and you are under the peculiar protection of the Lord Almighty. He hath plucked you as brands out of the burning, and redeemed you to himfelf with the faving ftrength of his right arm. When the blacknefs of darknefs furrounded your dwellings; when the terror of his judgements encompaffed you for difobedience, by his light you walked through the region and valley of the fhadow of death. Although for a moment he turned his face from you, yet, in everlafting kindnefs, hath he gathered you from the world to himfelf. Oh! may you ever remember his unutterable mercy, and dedicate the remainder of your days to the honour of his name.

My fpirit falutes you, in the endeared affection of the gofpel of peace, as fellow-travellers towards the land of eternal reft, and wifhes your eftablifhment in righteoufnefs for ever;—that you may abide in holy patience the fiery trial of faith through-

D   out

out the days of your earthly pilgrimage, and become as fixed pillars in the celeftial building and houfe of God.

If you ftedfaftly abide in the word of faith, wherein you have been taught, neither the malice of men, nor the united powers of darknefs, fhall be able to pluck you out of the hands of him who is your judge, your king, your protector, your father, and everlafting friend. *As a garden inclofed* has he made you, in fafe dwellings has he appointed your lots, and, in the end of days, he will be your refuge for ever. When this earth fhall be wrapped together like a fcroll, and the fun and moon be darkened; when every glorious conftellation of the heavens fhall fink into everlafting obfcurity, and the elements of this world fhall be diffolved with fervent heat; you will poffefs a habitation within the fuperior regions of a new heaven and a new earth, where the Lord your righteoufnefs dwells.

Many of the pretended wife, learned, and prudent, of this world, who have fought

to

to climb up fome other way rather than enter by Chrift, who is the door into the
fheepfold, may pity you as fools, or ridi-
cule you as enthufiafts; they may account
your life madnefs, and your end without
honour ; but they will one day be aftonifh-
ed at the ftrangenefs of your falvation,
when they may fee, to their confufion, that
you are finally numbered among the children of God, and your inheritance is a-
mong the faints.

In the world you are to expect tribula-
tions of various kinds, ficknefs, difeafe, and
pain : temptations and difappointments in-
vade the breafts of the moft temperate, virtuous, and religious, among men. A
cup of mixture, more or lefs impregnated
with the wormwood and the gall, is the
lot of humanity, defigned doubtlefs to effect a valuable purpofe by him who afflicts,
not willingly, nor without a righteous and
benevolent caufe, the children of men.

As

As the heavens are higher than the earth, so are the ways of the Almighty than our ways, and his thoughts than our thoughts.

We fee a little, and but a very little, of the amazing univerfal plan of his government over rational and immortal fpirits. It lies beyond the reach of the moft exalted created faculties to comprehend his wifdom throughout the righteous adminiftration of his providence, which is unfearchable. It is our duty, as frail, dependent, and impotent, beings, to meet every difpenfation with that refignation of fpirit which inceffantly breathes the humble language of *Not my will, O Lord, but thine, be done in all things.* Though the times are gloomy, the out-goings of the morning are of God. He will yet comfort the wafte places of Zion, and build up her defolations. He will make her wildernefs as Eden, and her deferts as the garden of the Lord : joy and gladnefs fhall be found therein, thankfgiving and the voice of melody. Awake, therefore,

fore, and put on ſtrength, ye who have *lien amongſt the pots*; ye, who have been afflicted, toſſed with tempeſts, and not comforted; for, the hour of your ſalvation is near. Abide in holy patience, and hope to the end. It is our duty, under the evils which we feel, and which our prudence could not prevent, to implore divine aid to endure them with patience, rather than to pray that they may be removed from us; leſt, like ignorant children, we ſhould ſeek to avoid that potion, from our heavenly Father's hand, which is gracۦouſly deſigned to remove, or prevent, a greater evil. This is not the place of your reſt, but a ſtate of probation, a painful pilgrimage, a land of pits and of ſnares, through which lies a narrow path to the regions of eternal peace. The ſoul, by reaſon of its connection with the body, and while incloſed within the walls of fleſh, cannot extend its views, and employ its faculties, on divine objects without frequent interruption. But, when the days of its captivity are accompliſhed, it

D 3　　　　　　　　will

will be capable of a more glorious expanfion in the kingdom of light and immortality, and poffefs that joy which is unfpeakable and full of glory. Therefore, in all the calamities to which we are fubject in the houfe of our pilgrimage, we have a place of refuge to flee to, where fafety is alone to be found. Though, indeed, we muft feel in fome degree as men, yet we may poffefs the patience, refignation, and holy fortitude, of Chriftians, who are looking for a better country, a more excellent inheritance, in that city whofe inhabitants have no occafion to complain that they are fick.

Be ye, therefore, ftedfaft, immoveable, always abounding in the work of the Lord, forafmuch as ye know that your labour fhall not be in vain. Be ye, in your feveral ftations in the church and in the world, as way-marks to the honeft fincere inquirers, who are afking the way to Zion, and, from a true fenfe of their condition, are crying out, *What fhall we do to be faved!* Shew forth, by your example of charity, fobriety,

briety, temperance, and holinefs of life, that you are redeemed from the fpirit of the world that lies in wickednefs. Be not captivated by its trifling amufements, nor enfnared by its lying vanities, but retain the fear of God, which will keep the heart clean, and prove a fource of fureft confolation when all things elfe will be unavailing. Let the purity of your lives demonftrate that you are attentive to things more excellent, and have placed your affections on things permanent and eternal ; things which effentially relate to the falvation of the foul.

Thus, you will be a means of leading others in the way of truth and righteoufnefs, and become the confecrated temples of the Holy Ghoft. You will witnefs an increafe of ftrength, wifdom, and holy ftability, from day to day, and perfeverance in the way that is everlafting.

Finally, my brethren, farewel. I commend you to God, the great Shepherd of Ifrael, and to the word of his grace, as the only

D 4　　　　　　infallible

infallible guide to direct you *What ye fhall do to be faved.* It is able to build you up in the moft holy faith, to direct your feet in the paths of righteoufnefs and peace, and, finally, to put you in poffeffion of a glorious inheritance, among the faints, that will never fade away !

DISCOURSE

DISCOURSE II.

*T*HEN *Jefus faid to his difciples, a rich man fhall hardly enter into the kingdom of heaven ; and again I fay unto you, it is eafier for a camel to go through the eye of a needle than for a rich man to enter into the kingdom of God. When his difciples heard it, they were exceedingly amazed, faying, who then can be faved ?* It is no wonder, indeed, that thefe appeared to them to be *hard fayings*, and that they fhould excite their aftonifhment, if they apprehended by them, that the kingdom of heaven was only open to poverty and wretchednefs. It appears, I think, beyond

controverfy,

controversy, that, notwithstanding the disciples attended to the doctrine of such an excellent minister, who spoke with peculiar authority, yet they did not at once comprehend the whole of his doctrine and works. Their understandings were gradually opened and informed : they were led on step by step. The work of religion was not with them, as some people have imagined the work of religion to be, an instantaneous work: they went on from strength to strength, and from one degree of knowledge to another, till they had acquired as much as was necessary for them. They were not instructed in all truths, but in such as respected the duties of their day and of their station, and which, in the course of their pilgrimage in this world, filled them with a humble hope and expectation of ultimately entering into one that is infinitely better, there to partake of the joy of their Lord, and of that rest from their labours which is prepared for the people of God. Thus, we find, when they

were

were told that *they muſt eat his fleſh, and drink his blood,* — that it was neceſſary a man ſhould *hate his father and mother, his wife, his children, and even his own life,* —accepting theſe texts, at firſt, in a ſtrict and literal ſenſe, it is no wonder they ſhould think them *hard ſayings :* hard indeed it would be if it were neceſſary that the affections, which flow from conſanguinity and affinity, muſt be totally eradicated, and the malignant paſſion of hatred be ſubſtituted, in order to render us ſuccefsful candidates for an inheritance that is incorruptible and that fadeth not away.

But it is clear to me, beyond the leaſt doubt, that our Lord deſigned, throughout the whole of his miniſtry, to excite and to ſtrengthen, inſtead of weakening, thoſe bands by which ſociety is held together.

He deſigned to inſpire us with the moſt friendly affections, as the main, or principal, motive to the diſcharge of the various ſocial and relative duties : this appears to me to be comprehended in the ſecond commandment,

mandment, *Thou shalt love thy neighbour as thyself.* With respect to this particular passage of the New Testament, it may, perhaps, be profitable, at least to the younger part of this assembly, whose experience has not yet been much, and whose observations have been but transient, to advert a little to the occasion of these *hard sayings*, which excited the amazement of the disciples.

It seems there was a young man who had heard of the fame of Jesus ; who wanted to be instructed with respect to what measures were necessary for him to adopt and to pursue in order to inherit everlasting life. Urged by this desire, he makes an application unto Jesus, addressing him after this manner, *Good master, what good thing shall I do, that I may inherit eternal life?* Our saviour enumerated several of the commandments, to which he replied, and no doubt with the greatest degree of sincerity, *All these have I kept from my youth up, what lack I yet?* It appears that our Lord meant to bring his love and his virtue to a severe test.

teft. *One thing*, fays he, *thou lackeft*; *if thou wilt be perfect, fell that thou haft, and give to the poor*; *take up thy crofs, and follow me, and thou fhalt have treafure in heaven.* It feems that our Saviour ftruck at his darling paffion, the love of money; for, upon hearing this propofal, it is evident that he preferred, at that time, retaining his corporeal poffeffions, that prefent temporary good, to the future and remote one of eternal life, for, *he went away forrowful.*

Then Jefus faid to his difciples, *A rich man fhall hardly enter into the kingdom of heaven.* It muft, indeed, be acknowledged, that, feeing we have nothing which we have not received, — that we are not proprietors of the inheritance which we poffefs, but tenants only at will; for, *the earth is the Lord's, and the fulnefs thereof, and the cattle on a thoufand hills,*—we ought to relinquifh, to give up, a part, or the whole, of that which is lent us, when it is the will of the giver to make that requifition : but it is evident to me, that this particular requifition

requifition intends not a general command. I conceive, that it is not riches, merely as riches, which can prevent our entrance into the kingdom of heaven. It may be faid, with equal truth, that *it is eafier for a camel to go through the eye of a needle than for a poor man to enter into the kingdom of heaven*, if he have nothing but poverty and wretchednefs to recommend him. It is very evident, from divers circumftances, that our Lord's controverfy was not with riches, but the fpirit of pride, which too frequently poffeffes the hearts of the rich ; for, we have an account of a rich, and yet of a good, man, Jofeph of Arimathea. From the feveral accounts of the evangelifts it appears he was an honourable counfellor, a rich man, a good, a juft, man, a difciple of Jefus, and one that *waited for the kingdom of God*, though it was probable that he was a member of the Sanhedrim.

It feems to me that the rich man, defigned in this text, is fuch a man as is reprefented to us in the parable : *There was a*
certain

certain rich man, who was clothed with pur-
ple and fine linen, and fared sumptuously every
day : there was also a certain beggar, that was
laid at his gate, full of sores, of whom there
can be no doubt that he was a proper object of human sympathy. He was laid at
his gate full of sores : his requisition was
humble, desiring to be fed only with *the*
crumbs that fell from the rich man's table ;
moreover, the dogs came and licked his sores.
It came to pass that the beggar died, and that
he was carried by the angels into Abraham's
bosom : the rich man also died, and was bu-
ried ; and he lifted up his eyes in hell, and
saw Lazarus in Abraham's bosom. He cried
out, in a sort of agony, Father Abraham, have
mercy upon me, and send Lazarus that he may
dip his finger in water to cool my tongue, for I
am tormented in this flame : but Abraham
answered, Son, remember, that thou, in thy life-
time, receivedst thy good things, and likewise
Lazarus evil things ; but now, he is comforted,
and thou art tormented. But we are not to
infer from this text, that, merely his being
clothed

clothed in purple and fine linen, or fáring fumptuoufly, was the caufe of his confequent mifery ; or, that it followed of courfe, having received the good things of this life, he fhould fuffer the worft of evils in the next ; but it appears he wanted that brotherly fympathy, that friendly affection, recommended to us in the character of the good Samaritan, which is not reftricted to any peculiar clafs, but directed to every object of diftrefs. There was a man, who, travelling from Jerufalem to Jericho, fell among thieves : he was fpoiled, he was wounded.—The prieft paffed by,—he who attended at the altar of God, he that fhould have poffeffed a fpirit of univerfal charity. The prieft paffed by,—the Levite followed his example, untouched with the feelings of humanity ; his heart was contracted, perhaps, by the prejudices of a party, which he had conceived to be religion. But a Samaritan paffed that way : he looked upon the man with that fympathy and compaffion which the love of Chrift infpires towards

wards a brother in diftrefs, incapable of relieving himfelf, upon whom many fuffe-rings were brought, and many more ex-pected to follow. He takes compaffion of this poor Jew, pours oil and wine into his wounds, attempts to alleviate his grief by leffening its caufe; and, though he could have no expectation of compenfation, yet it did not reftrain him from attempting e-very thing in his power for the relief of this indigent perfon, and his views were not confined to the prefent time; he look-ed forward, and endeavoured to provide for his future well-being, giving a direction unto his hoft, *I will repay thee*. It was there-fore the want of this fympathy, together with the fpirit of pride, which prompted the rich man to purfue the lufts of the flefh, of the eye, and the pride of life, at the ex-pence of his focial and religious duties, which rendered him highly criminal. This appears clearly to have been defigned : the character of this *certain rich man* and that of the beggar formed a contraft. The rich

E   man

man wanted virtue ; the poor man was deſtitute of food ; it is evident, however, that
he was in a humble ſtate. What could he
have aſked leſs if he had aſked any thing ?
The ſeverity of hunger forced him to aſk
thus much of him, as he was incapable of
helping himſelf. He .deſired only the
crumbs that fell from the rich man's table,
but he was unnoticed. If he had been of
the rich, if there had been a, proſpect that
the interest, or the pleaſure, of the rich
man could have been augmented by relieving him, he would have noticed him as La-
ban did Abraham's ſervant when he ſaw the
bracelets on his ſiſter's hands, *Come in, thou
bleſſed of the Lord, wherefore ſtandeſt thou
without ?* the door would have been readily opened to opulence, and titular dignity
would have found an eaſy acceſs ; but the
poor beggar lay unnoticed : the inferior
ſpecies of animals ſeemed to feel more ſympathy than the rich man, *Moreover the dogs
came and licked his ſores.* I would not be
underſtood, by any thing that I have ſaid,

to

to attempt an ingenious apology for the rich; but, at the same time, I would attempt to make that distinction between the poverty of the heart and the possessions of the hands which the author of the Christian religion designed. In the course of the providence of Almighty God it so falleth out, that the efforts of the laborious and industrious are not crowned with equal success. But we are not to conclude that the person, whose barns are filled with plenty, and whose presses are ready to burst *with new wine*, is the distinguished favourite of heaven, any more than that the poor man, who divides his morsel with his family, and mixes his tears with his bread, is reprobated by heaven. It is the abuse, and not the use, of riches which the testimony of Christ is certainly against. The apostles did not enjoin the rich to throw away their riches, but he exhorts Timothy to *charge them, who are rich in this world, that they be not high-minded,* that they assume nothing on the score of their possessions; *charge the*

rich

rich of this world that they be not high-minded, neither truft in uncertain riches, but in the living God, who giveth us all things richly to enjoy. This is what he had in charge, adding, I think, that *we brought nothing with us into the world, and we fhall carry nothing out of it.* *Naked we came into the world, naked we fhall return,* be diffolved and mixed with thofe elements, from which we originally fprang. I would, therefore, attempt, at leaft, that we fhould individually refleƈt upon the circumftances that we are placed in, and that we fhould receive with gratitude the portion which, in the general courfe of God's providence, fhall be allotted to us. Nothing more is required of us than to be *good ftewards of the manifold grace of God.* We are called ftewards ; and a time approaches, with unavoidable certainty, when the Lord of the univerfe will call us, will fummon us hence, with *give thou an account of thy ftewardfhip, for thou fhalt be no longer fteward.* Let us therefore confider the feveral talents we have received for the im-

provement

provement of our hearts in the Chriftian life : let us confider the outward benefits that are beftowed upon us, and let it be the ftudy of our lives to apply them properly, and to refemble the good Samaritan; that, in imitating the example of the author of the Chriftian religion, it may be the delight of our lives to diffufe happinefs all around, and to go *about doing good*. This appears to be of indifpenfible obligation. If the rich man had poffeffed this friendly difpofition, the beggar would not have been neglefted at the gates of his houfe, the dogs would not have been fuffered to lick his fores ; he would have poured into them lenient balm ; he would have attempted to bind up his broken heart, and to *wipe away all tears from all faces*, to diffufe happinefs in as extenfive a manner as his abilities could qualify him to diffufe it, and therein he would have been the beft prepared to join the heavenly fociety above, when a period fhould have been put to his exiftence upon earth, and his poffeffions could no

E 3   longer

longer avail him. But this was not the circumstance of the rich man ; he wanted *bowels of compaſſion* ; and, therefore, whatever religious party he was connected with, whether of the Phariſees or of the Sadducees, he was not acceptable in the ſight of the Searcher of hearts. Let us now reflect a little on what his feelings muſt be,—the feelings of a man that has rolled along in pomp, that has been clad *in purple and fine linen*, that has had his *ſinging men* and his *ſinging women*, with the ſound of the pipe and of the tabret, to attune his heart to joy, yet deſtitute of the feelings of humanity and of worthy ſentiments of religion. Death approaches,—he ſees the *heavens paſſing away as a ſcroll*, and the very foundation of his happineſs diſſolved. I cannot better expreſs it than in the language of the holy ſcriptures : *When in his proſperity, the deſtroyer came upon him ; his purpoſes were cut off, even the thoughts of his heart and the deſire of his eyes ; but his day is turned into night, his light into darkneſs ; his harp is turned into mourning,*

mourning, and his organ into the voice of them that weep. He is about to quit this scene of things without any hope or expectation of entering upon any scene that is better. He looks back upon a life that has been spent in various species of diffipation, in the gratification of his fenfual appetites, and in the neglect of every focial duty. He now finds himfelf in a circumftance far beneath the poor beggar's that lay at his gate.—Confcience refumes the feat fhe had loft,—wounds that had been healed break out afrefh, and bleed anguifh. He looks back, but it gives him no pleafure; the picture excites the moft painful feelings. He looks forward, but he has, no hope; his *finging men* and his *finging women*, with the voice of the pipe and the tabret, can no more infpire his foul with joy. He is about to quit this mortal ftage, and to enter into the world of fpirits, but deftitute of thofe moral virtues that would have qualified him to join the celeftial fociety, and to take a part in the general feftivity which

E 4 prevails

prevails throughout heaven's empire. The rich man lifted up his eyes to heaven in a state of anguish ; he beheld the beggar in Abraham's bosom. We are not to consider this text literally : this is a parable, not a matter of fact; and a parable designed to illustrate the moral doctrine of the gospel of Christ. He reaped the fruit of his doings, that which will inevitably follow a course of dissipation and a neglect of our proper duties : *The recompence of his hands* will be rendered to every man. *To those, who obey not the truth, but obey unrighteousness, indignation and wrath, tribulation and anguish, upon every soul of man that doeth evil : of the Jew first, and also of the Gentile ; for, there is no respect of persons with God:* and I wish to God there were less respect of persons with men. This was the circumstance, as I conceive, of the rich man.— Let us now consider what might be the feelings and the hopes of the poor beggar. Despised of his brethren, unpitied, unrelieved, he lay at the gates of the rich man ;

the

the dogs licked his wounds :—he importuned charity, — but he importuned in vain.
The rich man's ear was deaf to his prayers.
What confolation could he have in this
ftate ! Indeed, his feelings muft have been
exquifite. Hunger and thirft are appetites,
which, in the extreme, throw the mind into tumult. His natural feelings were painful, but what were his profpects ! What
were his hopes ! Though he was poor, he
was not forfaken of his Maker : he could
not boaft of *purple and fine linen*, he attended not the tables of the rich, nor partook
of their luxurious banquets, yet he was the
offspring of the eternal Father, who made
of *one blood all the nations of men who dwell
on all the face of the earth, and hath determined the bounds of their habitation.* If the
earth was unpropitious to his prayers, ftill
heaven was open to his cries. The Sovereign of the univerfe, who regards the *crying of the poor and the fupplication of the needy,*
took compaffion on the poor beggar. He
was about to quit his rags, to quit his poverty,

verty, and to enter into a state of everlasting happiness,—he was *carried by the angels
into Abraham's bosom.* Which of those cir-.
cumstances was the most desirable! Let us
extend our views beyond the present scene
of things: let us anticipate the shock we
cannot shun. Which would you rather
sustain, the character of this poor beggar,
or the character of *this certain rich man?*
Would you lose the hopes of the beggar in
order to sustain the dignity of the rich
man? This, methinks, is a question
which common sense would not be long in
deciding upon ; but, such is the weakness .
and frailty of our nature, that we approve
the right, and yet pursue the wrong : we
do the thing that we would not, and neglect
that which we would, do. The passions of
human nature are exceedingly strong, and
there is some one that generally characterises e-
very person ; a kind of reigning passion, which
like Aaron's rod, swallows up all the rest.
We are not all pursuing one path of vanity,
for its paths are endless : but we have an
aptitude,

aptitude, we have a promptnefs, rather to pursue measures that may produce a temporal good than those which will produce a spiritual good. The gratification of the present moment engages our passions. If we were to form an idea by the general practice of mankind, we seem to forget that we are mortal, and that we must die. Mankind busy themselves often beside their proper busines; and, whilst they are enlarging the boundaries of their earthly inheritance, are but little solicitous to obtain a habitation in the *new heavens and in the new earth, wherein righteousnefs dwells*. They prefer present to everlasting good, and neglect to cultivate those virtues which would make them resemble the Deity, (if I may be allowed the expreffion,) expand the faculties of the foul, and make it more capable of those fublime contemplations which are the employment of the celestial choir. I wish, therefore, that we might be induced to reflect on the vanity of human wishes, and on the folly of human purfuits. We have

no continuing city here : perfect felicity is
no more to be found in this mutable ftate
of things than it was practicable for the Ba-
bel builders to erect an edifice that fhould
reach the heavens. Many have foared a-
loft, and built their nefts on high, as upon
the cedar of Lebanon, yet they have been
brought down. Death levels all diftinctions, and earthly poffeffions make no diffe-
rence in the grave : let us fet our affections
therefore upon things that are above, and
not on things which are beneath. If our
affections be placed upon the fuperior good,
we fhall feel gradually a lefs attachment to
things that are feen ; — lefs to this world,
the fafhion whereof is paffing away, and
we are paffing away with it. Its pleafures
are but as a cloud, or a vapour, which will
foon difappear. We are haftening to the
place of our deftination, let us therefore
run with patience the race that is fet before us,
imitating the example of the wife and virtuous of all generations, endeavouring to
fulfil the various obligations that we are
under

under to the Author of our being and one
to another ;—to adopt the phrafe in the parable, that we *may be carried by angels into
Abraham's bofom*, and enter into the fulnefs
of that joy of which we have here but a
foretafte, as of the *brook that is by the way.*

Perhaps fome prefent, in the hours
of their folitude, may reflect, that they
pafs unnoticed amidft the throng, while
others fuftain the plaudit of the people.
Let them confider, that, in a few days,
there will be an end put to their anxie-
ties : if they be virtuous, indeed, they are
deftined for the regions of glory, immortality, and eternal life,— regions of which we
can at prefent form no adequate idea. We
fee but *darkly, as through a glafs,*—we explore
but a little of that vaft plan of the providential government of the fupreme Being ;
yet, in a future ftate, with faculties better
difpofed, with minds properly prepared, it
may be a part of our employment to inveftigate the difpenfations of divine providence, which at prefent appear exceedingly
myfterious ;

myſterious;—to celebrate, in a future world, the wonderful diſplay of wiſdom and power in the conſtitution of this, and alſo the goodneſs of God in adapting all his diſpenſations to all his people for the accompliſhment of their ſupreme good ; and, from a principle of conviction, to join the heavenly hoſt in ſaying, *Great and marvellous are thy works, Lord God Almighty: juſt and true are all thy ways, thou King of ſaints.* I am encouraged to expect this from the ſaying of Chriſt, that *what I do, thou knoweſt not now, but ſhalt know hereafter* ; therefore, let not the poor be diſconſolate in their habitations of poverty, but let them attempt, in their reſpective ſtations, to fill up the duties of their day, and they ſhall end in peace everlaſting. I intend not by what I have ſaid that I have any perſon in view who is wanting in charity and benevolence ; by no means : my deſign is general. I commend that good and virtuous diſpoſition which has been apparent in many whom I am addreſſing ; and I wiſh they may perſevere in

that

that which is right, and that they may endeavour *to lay up for themfelves a good foundation againft the time to come.* Riches are
attended with many fnares, and fo is poverty : that poverty, which brings a man to
want the neceffaries of life, will require uncommon fortitude and patience to bear.
There are indeed fnares in every ftate. E-
very ftate is a ftate of probation, and there
are temptations excited in our minds which
correfpond with the ftate and circumftances
that we are in, and to the feveral biaffes
that we poffefs. Let us therefore *lay, afide
every weight and burden, and the fin which eafily befets us, and run with patience the race
that is fet before us,* cherifhing, in the firft
inftance, a fincere love of the fupreme Being in the higheft degree, and then the love
of our neighbour as ourfelves, that we may
poffefs a fpirit of univerfal benevolence,
which will prompt us to do all the good we
can to that family of which the Lord God
Almighty is the Father and Head. I conceive, indeed, that religion and virtue allow

of

of degrees in love. There are peculiar at-
tachments which arife from confanguinity;
and alfo from affinity, which religion has
no controverfies with. We read, in the character of our Lord, that, notwithftanding
he poffeffed a *love of all* his difciples, and of
all the inhabitants of the earth, yet John
feemed to be diftinguifhed : *he leaned upon
his bofom*, he was the difciple whom Jefus
loved; but we are not hence to conclude
that he loved no other ; but there was a
peculiar attachment to the *difciple whom Jefus loved*.

I would recommend, in attempting
every ftep of reformation, and in every
good word and work, that we attend to,
and wait for, the influence of the holy Spirit ; that which would fanctify us, that
which would gradually inform our underftandings, remove our prejudices and our
doubts, infpire us with the moft fubftantial hopes, and open to us profpects that
are the moft pleafing ; and, whatever portion of ill may be allotted us in the courfe
of divine providence, let the virtuous ever
bear

bear in remembrance that *there is a river,*
the ſtreams whereof make glad the heritage
of God ; and every ſincere devoted ſoul, of
every nation, kindred, tongue, and people,
that fears God and works righteouſneſs, is
part of this heritage, which is repleniſhed
with the ſhowers of immortal goodneſs,
and is as a *garden incloſed,* notwithſtanding
the different circumſtance of individuals.
The whole of this heritage is incloſed with
walls that are impregnable, — impregnable
againſt the enemy. They will be preſerved,
by the providence of Almighty God, as in
a garden that is incloſed, — a garden that
will be refreſhed with the deſcent of celeſtial rain, that will be repleniſhed, and bring
forth the acceptable fruits of virtue and holineſs. *My ſoul,* ſaith the Pſalmiſt, *thirſt-*
eth for God ; *yea, for the living God* ; and a-
gain, *As the heart panteth for the water-*
brooks, ſo panteth my ſoul after thee, O God !
This is the diſpoſition of the humble ſoul,
who looks upon the Lord as his ſuperior
good, and prefers a communion with him

F   to

to the *increafe of corn, wine, or oil.* He will, by every method, endeavour to keep open a communication with this fountain, — a fountain that will never be exhaufted. Thanks be to God *we have a river*: though we may be expofed to many things, to the darknefs and light, the heat and the cold, yet, in the courfe of our pilgrimage, there is a river that flows from Hermon's hills, the ftreams whereof ever make glad the heritage of God.

Let us attempt to pafs along this river that we may be replenifhed, fo fhall we experience that which is fpoken of Wifdom, *my brook became a river, and my river became a fea.* The good, the virtuous, man; the man, that feels the emotions of filial piety, has recourfe to this river. A brook is opened to him by the way, at which he can fatiate his thirft, and renew his ftrength. He will, in waiting upon God, *mount up as on wings of an eagle, he will walk, and not be weary; run, and not be faint.* Thanks be to God that we have this river, and I wifh

we

we may diftinguifh this *fountain of living water* from the *broken cifterns that can hold no water*. If this be the cafe with our hearts, then we fhall find our confolation enlarge, our hopes increafe till they are loft in fruition, and our faith terminate in open vifion, in the contemplation of thofe truths of which we can at prefent form but inadequate ideas, when we fhall enter into the joy of our Lord, and be numbered with the wife. *They that are wife fhall fhine as the brightnefs of the firmament, and they that turn many to righteoufnefs as the ftars for ever and ever !*

THE

THE

PRAYER

AT THE

CONCLUSION of the MEETING.

MOST Gracious God, inspire our
hearts with suitable reverence, that
we may approach thee acceptably, and offer up our prayers to thee in full assurance
that, though heaven is thy throne, and the
earth thy footstool, yet thou art graciously
pleased to notice the inhabitants of this
lower

lower world, as well as thofe who are clothed with the greateft degree of dignity, and are perfectly happy in a world that is infinitely fuperior. Imprefs our hearts with a fenfe of thy goodnefs, upon which we every moment depend. Let it be manifefted unto us, that the difpenfing of thy manifold grace fhould imprefs us with emotions of filial piety and gratitude unto thee, who art the fource of every thing that is good. We approach thy altar in the multitude of thy mercies, and look in confidence towards thee, that, notwithftanding our many infirmities, *there is mercy with thee, that thou mayeft be feared.* Grant, we befeech thee, that, by the operation of thy holy Spirit, thou everlafting Shepherd and Bifhop of fouls, multitudes may be gathered out of the wildernefs, in which they have wandered and been loft, within thy fold, to become a part of thy flock, and the fheep of thy pafture. Be pleafed, in mercy, to bring back every fheep that has ftrayed unto the fold again, that, as we are thine by

F 3   creation,

creation, we may, at length, be thine by adoption into a ſtate of ſonſhip, and become heirs of a ſpiritual inheritance, the crown immortal, that ſhall never fade away.

O moſt righteous and everlaſting Father, be pleaſed, we humbly beſeech thee, to look down upon the various circumſtances of thy people ; conſole the poor, and abate the pride of the rich, that we may, by the interpoſition of thy ſpirit, be what thou wouldſt have us to be, a humble dependent people, looking up unto thee as the ſource whence all our bleſſings are derived, and imploring at thy throne to be inſtructed to uſe our talents to the ends and purpoſes for which thou haſt given them, that, when ever thou ſhalt be pleaſed to ſummon us hence, we may have an evidence, a hope, as an anchor that is moſt ſure and ſtedfaſt, that may preſerve our ſouls in tranquillity when the waves of affliction roar, when the winds of adverſity may blow upon us from every quarter. In the moſt painful diſpenſations

fations we may have to pafs through, grant
that we may find an afylum in thy name,
which has been the tower of defence, the mu-
nition of rocks, to the righteous in all generations.

O Lord, enable us to call fuccefsfully upon thy name, that we may be faved with
an everlafting falvation ; that, fortified by
thy grace, we may endure the dangers of
profperity, and alfo the trials of poverty,
if they fhall be permitted to attend us ;
that we may not be elevated too high, nor
puffed up to deny thee, and fay, who is the
Lord ? nor may be ever fo caft down and
oppreffed in adverfity, as to fteal, and take
thy name in vain, to deny thee, O God ;
but that, in every difpenfation of thy providence, we may humbly acquiefce with
thy will, and fay, *Not my will, O Lord, but
thine be done.*

Grant, we befeech thee, that, under an
awful fenfe of thy attributes, which it is
not in the power of human beings adequate-
ly to conceive, nor of the tongues of an-

gels

gels to exprefs, in the contemplation of thy attributes, our fouls, inflamed with a fpirit of pure devotion, may afcend up, and put up our fupplications, to thee, O Lord. We feel a holy awe pervade our fouls : in the contemplation of thy attributes our words are fwallowed up : we offer unto thee the increafe of praife, and afcribe unto thee every thing that is excellent, every thing that is great : to thee belong majefty and dominion, with every other adorable attribute, now and for evermore. Amen.

DISCOURSE

DISCOURSE III.

THERE is part of a pfalm, or hymn, compofed by a fervant of God, which has been revived, in my remembrance, in this meeting; and I may fay, in much fincerity, it hath been the language of my heart : *Offer unto God thankfgiving.*

The defign of the author of this pfalm was, to excite, both in himfelf and in the minds of others, the moft fervent emotions of gratitude, thankfgiving, and praife. Thankfgiving, if it be more than the cold

formality

formality of unmeaning words, is the genuine offspring of gratitude and devotion.
It arifes from a juſt fenſe of the manifold
favours beſtowed upon us by the providence
of God, who hath liberally fupplied his
creatures with the proviſion neceſſary for
‘them.

The Scriptures fpeak of the Almighty
not only as watching over, and providing
for, the fuperior clafs of beings in this
world, but as extending his providential
care (to uſe a comparative mode of fpeech)
to the meaneſt of his creatures. Not a
fparrow falls without him : he heareth the
young ravens when they cry, and he hath
provided richly for the foul of every living
thing. Man, in a peculiar manner, appears
to be diſtinguiſhed above all other claſſes of
animal exiſtence by a rational power of reflection. He is capable of afcending from
effect to caufe, of obferving the concatena-
tion thereof, and of inferring, from the
phænomena of nature, the exiſtence of a
wife, powerful, intelligent, and good, Being

ing, whom we call God. Hence he becomes an accountable creature : hence he
has a motive to thankſgiving and praiſe, of
which the lower orders of animals are not
capable ; for, whatever ſimilarity there may
be between the endowments of inferior animals, and their inſtinctive powers, and the
faculties of the human ſpecies, yet hiſtory
affords us no inſtance of the former betray-
ing the leaſt ſigns of devotion. Man is
made a little, and perhaps but a little, lower than the angels. He is capable of contemplating the attributes of the ſupreme
Cauſe ; and who can contemplate the attributes of the divine Being without feeling the emotions of filial fear and gratitude ? But it is exceedingly to be regretted,
that we uſe not thoſe ſuperior powers, with
which we are endued to the nobleſt purpoſes, for which they were given us. We
employ too little of the ſhort ſpan of time
in the inveſtigation of ſubjects which are
adapted to inſpire us with the beſt affections, and to acquire thoſe virtues that
would

would dignify our nature: but, inftead thereof, we defcend from the rank we fhould fill, and, with inferior orders of a-nimals, make paffion, inftead of right rea-fon, our guide and ruler. Thus we be-come governed by thofe fenfual appetites which we fhould govern. We give away the power received for the nobleft purpo-fes, or make it fubfervient to our loweft paffions; and, like thofe animals which are fed by fruit which drops fpontaneoufly from the trees, fome people feem deftitute of reflection whence their provifion is deri-ved, feldom look up, feldom, if ever, con-template the caufe, feldom reflect *that the earth is the Lord's, and the fulnefs thereof, with the cattle on a thoufand hills*, and that we are every moment dependent on his bounty. This is the unhappy circumftance of too many of the fons and daughters of men.

I apprehend the principal defign of all Gofpel minifters is, to excite in the minds of their hearers fuch reflections, on beings circumftanced

circumftanced as we are, and on the relation we bear one to another and to the fupreme Caufe, as may be productive of filial piety, prompt us to make our hearts
the facred altar of the Lord Almighty, and
offer unto God thankfgiving and praife.

I fervently wifh that all our hearts may
be at this feafon, and not only at this feafon
but at all other times, fo impreffed with
the infinite obligation we are under to the
fupreme Being, that thankfgiving might become an habitual frame of fpirit, continued
throughout all the occurrences of life, fetting the Lord always before our eyes that
we do not evil or offend him. Ingratitude,
it feems, actuated the children of Ifrael.
It hath been the principal caufe, or fource,
of all moral evil. Thus, the people of the
houfe of Ifrael received the favours of
heaven without turning their thoughts
reverently toward the fource whence
they were derived : *they ate and drank, and
rofe up to play.*

Inftead

Inſtead of being diſpoſed to thankſgiving, they indulged a ſpirit of levity. They rioted on the divine bounty, and forgot to give thanks: they wanted, therefore, a proper motive to the diſcharge of their ſeveral duties ; for, when we are impreſſed with a proper ſenſe of gratitude for favours received, we are naturally diſpoſed to ſearch for, or ſtudy, the will and pleaſure of the perſon who conferred on us thoſe favours. We carefully watch for an opportunity to expreſs our gratitude, not only in being verbally thankful, but are alſo ſtudious to avoid every thing that would furniſh occaſion of offence to our benefactor ; and, on the other hand, are equally ſtudious to render ourſelves, as much as poſſible, worthy objects of his favourable regard. Thus it is in ſocial life among men, and ſimilar thereto it is with thoſe minds which are impreſſed with a ſenſe of gratitude to the ſupreme Being. The conſideration of his goodneſs ſhould lead us to reflect on our own unworthineſs ; for, we are indeed *unworthy*

worthy of the leaft of his mercies, and of his truth; yet he has favoured us with the former and the latter rain, the upper and the nether fprings; with feed-time and with harveft; has filled our barns with plenty, and hath liberally provided for the fuftenance of his creatures. Impreffed with the fenfe which this obligation impofes, the grateful heart would approach his altar in the multitude of his mercies, and fay, *What shall we render unto thee for thy goodnefs to the children of men?*

This is the language of the devoted heart; and, though it might be uttered only mentally, or not be expreffed by any vocal found, yet the Searcher of hearts would accept that affection, or devotion of mind. He accepts the intention of the heart before it is brought forth, or manifefted by any external act, and we fhall then have the moft powerful motive to hope for the divine aid. Were our hearts thus impreffed, we fhould embrace every opportunity of enquiring how we fhould commend our-

ourfelves to his notice, — how exprefs the gratitude we feel. We fhould be induced to manifeft it by a difcharge of every re-ligious and of every focial duty, by waiting upon and worfhipping him, by offering to him the pure incenfe of thankfgiving and praife, expreffing what we feel for the favours received, by communicating, in proportion to our refpective meafures, to thofe who ftand in need of affiftance; and, indeed, impreffed with the emotions of gratitude to God, it will be the chief plea-fure of our lives to *go about doing good* a-mong men. But of thofe, who are defti-tute of this moft worthy principle of grati-tude, other joys allure the affections, other motives than religious and focial duties. They are in purfuit of fome favourite fen-fual object, which, at beft, compared with the fuperior good, is only an unfubftantial phantom, and purfued at the expence of e-very thing that confers real dignity on a

rational

rational being, and renders him acceptable to the Judge of all the earth.

Thus the children of Ifrael, in proportion as they loft fight of the providence of the Almighty, and of what he had done for them, became more and more depraved; infomuch, that they joined fome of the furrounding nations in the performance of idolatrous acts. They feemed to have loft the idea of the unity of God : they became deftitute of a fpirit of gratitude. The prophet, in the name of the Lord, degrades them beneath the condition of the moft contemptible claffes of animals :· *Hear, O heavens, and give ear, O earth! for, the Lord hath fpoken, the ox knoweth his owner, and the afs his mafter's crib, but Ifrael doth not know, my people doth not confider.* If thefe animals are not capable of rational reflection, yet they poffefs fomething that bears a refemblance of gratitude, diftinguifhed by the appellation of *inftinct.* They, at leaft, exprefs fome notice of thofe on whom they depend for fupport : *the ox*

G   *knoweth*

knoweth his owner, and the afs his mafter's crib. This paffage fets forth the great moral depravity of that people; and, in fhort, the hiftory, which the holy Scriptures furnifh us with refpecting the children of Ifrael, conveys a charge of peculiar ignorance, obftinacy, and ingratitude: *The ox knoweth his owner, and the afs his mafter's crib; but Ifrael doth not know, my people doth not confider. Ah, finful nation, a people laden with iniquity, a feed of evil doers!* In another place, the prophet hath fhewn, that, in departing from what they fhould have been, in forfaking the God of their fathers, for want of a reverent attention to his ftatutes, they loft the fpirit of devotion, and judgements were inflicted on them by extraordinary caufes. They deprived themfelves of the felicity that is infinitely fuperior to all the gratifications of fenfual appetites. *My people have committed two evils; they have forfaken me, the Fountain of living waters, and have hewn to themfelves cifterns, broken cifterns, which can hold no water.* Here

again

again they are indirectly charged with ingratitude. To ufe the figurative language
of the holy Scriptures, *he fpread a table for
them in the wildernefs,* conducted them by a
cloud by day, and a pillar of fire by night,
put them into poffeffion of *vineyards which
were not theirs, and of olive-yards which they
had not planted,* yet they were ungrateful; they
ceafed to *offer unto God thankfgiving* ; that is
to fay, the fpecies of thankfgiving which is
acceptable to the fupreme Being. They
made, indeed, many prayers; they fpread
forth their hands toward the habitation of
his holinefs; the fervices of the tabernacle
were punctually performed; but, with all
thefe, they poffeffed not a fpirit of thankfgiving, but offered unto God a mere form of
words, fentiments in which the heart took
no part, which had not been dictated by a
fpirit of gratitude. They offered, therefore, the *facrifice of fools.* Such is the
weaknefs of our nature, that we would
perfuade ourfelves, were it poffible, that the
Almighty poffeffes the vanity and ambition

G 2   of

of a creature who is fond of the incenſe of adulation, and capable of being deceived by the offerings of flattery, in which the heart is not intereſted; but, as he is without the parts, ſo he is without the paſſions, of a creature. No weakneſs is to be attributed to him, who is perfeᶜt and ſelf-ſufficient. He can derive no additional felicity from our thankſgiving : he can experience no diminution from our withholding him the praiſe which is due to his great and excellent name. He has inſtituted worſhip, and commanded thankſgiving, for our ſakes, to promote our felicity, and not his own. Can we ſuppoſe, that, approaching him with words compoſed by way of prayer and thankſgiving, in which the heart is not intereſted, can be acceptable to him ? No : and therefore their new moons, the calling of their aſſemblies, and their many prayers, were not acceptable incenſe to the Lord God of Sabaoth. They had *committed two evils : they had forſaken him, the Fountain of living waters, and had hewn*

hewn unto themfelves cifterns, broken cifterns, which could hold no water. Therein is fet forth the great lofs that people fuftained when they departed in heart from that reverent attention which they fhould have paid to the fupreme Being while they were partakers of his favours and mercies; the great lofs they fuftained by forfaking the everlafting Fountain of felicity for the mere fenfual pleafures of this life, which are not to be compared with the fpiritual joys that refult from a ftate of real devotion and thankfgiving.

There is no fource of temporal pleafure but what may foon terminate. Difappointment awaits us in every ftate. Pains, afflictions, difeafes, may foon render us incapable of tafting thofe pleafures we have long been in the purfuit of; and, after a tedious chafe, in the moment when we blefs ourfelves with the expectation of fruition, we grafp the phantom, and find it air. How many inftances have we feen of people, intoxicated with a fpirit of ambition and ava-

rice,

rice, who fuppofed that the accumulation
of·wealth would render them perfectly happy; who have propofed to themfelves a future period, when they fhould fit down at
the end of their labours in peace; and have
gone on, from one ftage of life to another,
led as it were by an *ignis-fatuus*, to peram-
bulate the enchanted circle! Difappointment
has terminated their purfuits. If we have
not fomething elfe to reft our hopes upon
than the pleafure which this world can produce, we fhall be like the man who dreamt
that he was hungry, and ate; thirfty, and
he drank; but awoke, and beheld his appetites ftill remained: and this may perhaps
conftitute, in part, the mifery of a future
ftate,—the entering into it with appetites
which cannot be gratified.

Having attempted to fhew the importance of gratitude, and the difmal confe-
quences that flow from the contrary principle, I will now attempt, at leaft, to
point out one caufe why we feel fo little of
this virtuous affection; — that is, Ambition,

tion, the grand enemy of man's felicity. On the wings of imagination, in an extravagant anticipation of the future, man deprives himfelf of the enjoyment which virtue would yield him in the prefent hour. *He labours for very vanity, and difquiets himfelf in vain.* Perhaps we fhall find the very feeds of ambition fown as it were, and interwoven, with our very nature and conftitution. There is fome fpecies of ambition that takes place in the loweft as well as in the higheft ranks of fociety. In our prefent circumftances, let them be what they may above wanting the neceffaries of life, (which is the lot of but very few, comparatively fpeaking; and, of this few, the evil has been brought upon them principally by their own imprudence and intemperance,) we fhould be content. A few, indeed, have been fubjected to want the neceffaries of life by unavoidable events : thefe are worthy objects of charity, and will not be neglected by thofe who can feel for another's woe. But, indeed, fuch is

G 4   the

the want of fympathy, that fome people feldom fee an affliction without their own doors. They live for themfelves only, and feem as if they were as deftitute of the love of their neighbour as they are of gratitude to God. But, with refpect to this paffion of ambition, againft which I would in a peculiar manner endeavour to guard the minds of youth, refift it early, or it will grow with your growth, and ftrengthen with your ftrength. Guard againft the errors of libertinifm, the errors of the fpendthrift, and the errors of the mifer, that you may early poffefs the emotions of gratitude to the Author of your being. If it be your lot to abound in this world's goods, receive the fuperabundant favours with gratitude, and thankfully apply them to the purpofes for which they were given. But, fuch is the nature of this paffion, (ambition,) that it prompts us to look up to the claffes of mankind a little above us, and not to the Moft High. We look among our neighbours, who have acquired

a

a little more than we have acquired, and are led as it were imperceptibly towards a ſtate we can never attain. I have never known, in the courſe of my obſervation, a perſon, who was not contented in a low ſtate of life, that was ever happier in a higher; but I have known ſome who have been happy in a low ſtation, and, when they have eaten their morſel in quietneſs, have offered unto God thankſgiving and praiſe. Happineſs is tendered to all. Be but grateful, and thou ſhalt be happy; for, gratitude will inſpire us with this ſentiment, *Having food and raiment, be therewith content.*

I make theſe obſervations on the ſubject without premeditation; and, indeed, the want of order in my delivery of them will be a ſufficient proof of it. I recommend them to your ſerious conſideration, and wiſh your hearts may be ſuitably impreſſed with the ſubject. And, though thankſgiving ſhould be our general mental habit, our hearts ſhould be particularly impreſſed with
it

it at particular times. We ought to look up with peculiar thankſgiving to the throne of grace in the moment of fruition. We have enjoined no peculiar mode, or form, of prayer or thankſgiving. We have no ceremony by way of grace before and after meat; but, in diſpenſing with theſe forms, we do not diſpenſe with the thing itſelf intended by them. We ought to be impreſſed with filial piety towards our Almighty Father. We ought to make a ſolemn pauſe previous to our partaking of the divine bounty, and to poſſeſs ſuch a ſpirit of devotion, that we may *offer*, at leaſt mentally, *unto God thankſgiving and praiſe*.

And, at the cloſe of the day, though we have no form of evening or morning prayer, yet I would attempt to impreſs the minds of youth eſpecially, that, before they cloſe their eyes to ſleep, they ſhould review the tranſactions of the paſt day, and ſee what there is to approve, what to condemn,—to contemplate the mercy and the goodneſs extended to them, that they may

offer

offer unto God *thankfgiving* for his mercies,
and commend themfelves to his protection.
Again, in the morning, we ought alfo to
offer up thankfgiving. If we poffefs this
difpofition of mind, we fhall not be entan-
gled with the things of this life, which enfnare, but fhall confider ourfelves as ftrangers and pilgrims on earth, anticipating a
better country, a better inheritance, where,
with faints and angels, and the fpirits of
juft men made perfect, in a humble contemplation of the divine attributes, and of
the difpenfations of his providence, and favoured with the renewed impreffion of his
goodnefs, we may, with purified fpirits,
approach him in the multitude of his mercies, and *offer unto him thankfgiving and
praife !*

DISCOURSE

DISCOURSE IV.

ARISE, and go hence; for, this is not thy rest! We are abundantly inſtructed in the holy ſcriptures reſpecting the ſhortneſs of human life, the brevity of all terreſtrial pleaſures, and the vanity of all human purſuits, compared with the ſatiſfaction which is found in a courſe of virtue, and the glorious hope with which it inſpires its humble votaries of ultimately poſſeſſing

an

*an inheritance which is incorruptible, and
fadeth not away.*

It is the worthy purpose, or end, of real
religion, to ennoble our nature, to raife
our thoughts and contemplations from carnal to fpiritual, from terreftrial to celeftial,
objects. *Set your affections,* fays the apoftle, *on things above, not on things on the
earth.* If our affections be folely placed on
things which are beneath, or on the pleafures derived to us from an intercourfe with
the objects of fenfe, our happinefs, indeed,
will be exceedingly fhort-lived and uncertain. *Here we have no continuing city :* every thing of a terreftrial nature is mutable.
There is not any ftate or circumftance of
life, however pleafing, that we can have a-
ny fecurity will continue long.

A tranfition, from a ftate of opulence
to a ftate of poverty, our own obfervations
have inftructed us, has fometimes been
made very quick. We cannot either fore-
fee or prevent thofe occurrences which
may be productive in future of profperity

or

or adverſity, of pleaſure or pain. *The faſhion of this world*, ſaith the apoſtle, *paſſeth away*, and we are indeed paſſing with it. Short is the ſpan of human life : ſhort the path we have to tread from the cradle to the grave, the houſe appointed for the reception of all living; for, *duſt thou art, and to duſt thou ſhalt return*. Seeing, therefore, *we have no continuing city*, let us form the wiſe reſolution of ſeeking one that is to come; *a city which hath foundations, whoſe builder and maker is God*. I have underſtood by this paſſage of Scripture, which is figurative, that we are called upon, as rational creatures, by the voice of divine wiſdom, ſeeing all the pleaſures, or ſatisfactions, which ariſe from an intercourſe with ſenſible objects, muſt terminate, to endeavour, by the beſt uſe or application of thoſe powers, which heaven has endued us with, to ſeek that ſpecies of happineſs which will be permanent, and is adapted to the nature of a rational and an immortal ſpirit. This is the comment which I have made on this

paſſage

paffage of holy writ : and I do moft fervently
wifh that our minds may be difpofed at this
feafon ferioufly to reflect on the comparative
folly of all fenfual indulgences, and on the
vanity of human purfuits ; and be animated to feek the fuperior good, a habitation
in the *city of the faints folemnities, a city that
hath foundations. Look,* faith the text, *upon Zion, the city of our folemnities, and thine eyes
fhall fee Jerufalem a quiet habitation* ; *not one of
its ftakes fhall ever be removed, nor any of its
cords be broken :* there the *glorious Lord* is to
its inhabitants as *a place of broad rivers and
ftreams.* He is the fource whence their
happinefs is derived ; and, as he is immortal, the happinefs, derived from an intercourfe or communion with him will
confequently be permanent. We are inftructed by what means we are to feek fuccefsfully this *city that hath foundations.* We
are told, in the Revelations, in words fome-
what of this import, Bleffed is he who
keepeth the commandments of God : he
fhall have accefs to the tree of life, which
ftands

ftands in the midft of the Paradife of God, fhall enter in through the gates into the city, and become a fellow-citizen with the faints, and of the houfehold of God. Here we learn, that, if we would poffefs a habitation in this city, we muft feek it by walking in the commandments. Again, *if thou wilt enter into life, keep the commandments.* There is no other way to become an inhabitant of this city than by obedience to the facred commandments of heaven, which are of univerfal obligation. Let us not, therefore, expect to climb up any other way, or to attain a ftate of felicity hereafter, by any other mode than obedience from the heart to the manifeftations of the divine will ; and, with refpect to the commandments of God, we are alfo inftructed by what means they are to be afcertained ; at leaft, by individuals for themfelves : *a manifeftation of the Spirit is given to every man to profit withal.* It is called *light,* becaufe it hath a property which is analogous to that element. It illuminates the underftandings

H   of

of mankind, by inftructing them in matters of the greateft importance,—matters
which refpect their final acceptance with
the Judge of the whole earth at the laft
day.

But, though the light fhines, or *a manifeftation of the Spirit is given to every man to
profit withal*, yet there are, comparatively
fpeaking, but few who attend to its dictates, and purfue that courfe of virtue
which the light of the gofpel of Jefus evidently points out. It is with many as it
was with the multitude when our Lord
was perfonally on earth. *Light*, fays he, *is
come into the world, but men love darknefs rather than light*. He came, a divine meffenger of heaven, to propofe the terms of reconciliation to fallen creatures. He came
to enlighten their underftandings, to correct the depravity of their hearts, to purify them, and to make them meet for an *inheritance which is incorruptible, and fadeth
not away*. He came to reveal to them the
way which leads to this glorious city; but
they

they turned a deaf ear to the inftructions of wifdom : they would not attend to his coun-fel, nor be admonifhed by his reproofs. *Light is come into the world, but men love darknefs rather than light. They hate the light, neither come to the light, left their deeds fhould be reproved.*

Perhaps, if we review our lives ; if we look into the book of confcience, we fhall find fomething recorded there which bears a refemblance, more or lefs, to the circum-ftance of thofe people in the days of our Lord's perfonal appearance on earth. There is not a being, arrived to years capa-ble of ferious reflection, who hath not had fome fecret convictions for doing wrong; who hath not had fome compunction of confcience for having tranfgreffed the laws and ftatutes of heaven. But, as the point-ing of the facred finger leads to things con-trary to the wifh of the fenfual heart, im-merfed in pleafures derived from terref-trial purfuits, we are not difpofed to attend to the inftruction of the facred monitor.

We

We are rather difpofed to be flattered in our vices, to be foothed in our fins, than to have them correfted, and to be led into the juft man's path, *which is as the fhining light, that fhineth more and more unto the perfect day.*

There is a circumftance on record concerning an ancient king, which may ferve, perhaps, to illuftrate the doftrine which I have in view to affert. He was about to lead out his army to battle, and was doubtful of the event of his intended enterprife. He was defirous, if poffible, to know what fhould be the decifion of the day ; and, for that purpofe, he intended to confult fome feer ; but he meant fome perfon who fhould be capable of flattering his vanity and wifhes. A prophet of the Lord was propofed to him,—one who had never afted the part of a fycophant, but had fpoken the word of the Lord faithfully : — but he was not difpofed to confult this prophet. That, indeed, which would have recommended him to every judicious perfon, was the caufe

of

of his refufing to confult him. He knew he would not attempt to footh his vanity, prophefy fmooth things, or fpeak deceit: therefore he determined not to confult him. *I hate him, for he doth not prophefy good concerning me, but evil.* And thus, with refpect to the divine monitor, the manifeftation of the grace of God in the human heart, which bears a faithful teftimony to our confciences; we are not difpofed to attend to its dictates, but we call upon our paffions to footh us, to flatter us, and to concur with our vain hopes, and, by this means, have neglected things which are of the greateft importance. We are rather defirous that we may be indulged in the purfuit of lying vanities, than to have our eyes effectually opened to fee our own nakednefs, the depravity of our hearts, and the way which leads to Zion. *I hate him; for, he doth not fpeak good concerning me, but evil.* Thus mankind hate the reproofs of the divine light in their own confciences, becaufe it teftifies againft their darling paf-

H 3   fions,

fions, and thwarts them in their pleafing purfuits ; intercepts their long-indulged profpects, and points out to them a road, the purfuit of which would afford them no pleafure though it leads to Zion. Their thoughts are engroffed by inferior objects ; they have no tafte, or relifh, for things which are of a fpiritual nature, but would, if it were poffible, take up their reft in tranfient gratifications, and not be folici- tous with refpect to the conclufion of the fcene, or what fhall be their circumftance, or ftate, in the world, or life, which is to come.

They hate the light : why fo ? becaufe it manifefts their deeds of darknefs. They do not like to take a view of their own hearts. Such is the depravity thereof, that a view of it is indeed humiliating to the pride of human nature. They had rather draw a veil over their fins than fee them in their proper colours, as they really are ; or purfue fuch meafures of conduct as would ennoble their nature, rectify their

judge-

judgements, and open to them profpects far more inviting than what this world can afford, even the profpect of an everlafting habitation *in the new heaven and the new earth, wherein righteoufnefs dwells.*

But, though I am led to fpeak after this manner, I have no doubt that there are many in this audience who have weighed the worth of vanity, and eftimated the infignificancy of all terreftrial things ; who have feen that they are not adapted to fatiate the thirft of an immortal fpirit. They have contemplated, and have gathered from their own obfervations, that every thing is mutable ;— that the finger of Omnipotence hath written on the face of univerfal nature, *They fhall perifh.* They have gathered, I fay, from their own obfervations, that every thing, included in this fyftem, is mutable ; and that, in a fhort time, a period will be put to their exiftence on earth, when their connection with all fublunary objects will be diffolved for ever. Under fuch a profpect of the uncer-

H 4

tainty

tainty of terreftrial pleafures, they have been animated to *feek a city which hath foundations*; or, in other words, have been excited, by the pureft motives, to purfue thofe means which will introduce that happinefs into the foul which is not dependent on any elementary or fecondary caufes, but on an union of foul with the Author of its being ; and have chofen, if it fhould be their lot in the courfe of the providence of divine wifdom, to *fuffer rather affliction with the people of God, than to enjoy the pleafures of fin, which are but for a feafon.* I falute thefe with the falvation of the love of the gofpel of Chrift. Thefe are *feeking a city which hath foundations, whofe builder and maker is God*; and their hope will not be as the *hope of the hypocrite, which will perifh,* but a hope that will terminate in an everlafting fruition of joys, which eye *hath not feen, nor hath ear heard, nor hath it entered into the heart of man to conceive. Bleffed are they who keep the commandments of God : they will have accefs to the tree of life, which ftands in* the

the midſt of the Paradiſe of God, and ſhall enter in through the gates into the city,—become fellow-citizens with the ſaints, and of the houſehold of God. For, having been redeemed from the bondage of corruption, they ſhall enjoy the glorious liberty of the ſons of God; they ſhall enter into the city of the ſaints ſolemnities, the inhabitants whereof ſhall never complain that they are ſick. Indeed, it affords the moſt enlivening ſpecies of hope, to them that ſeek this city, that, when the clouds ſhall gather blackneſs, darkneſs, and tempeſt, — when the proſpect of the future ſhall be exceedingly gloomy,—they can penetrate this gloom, and anticipate an everlaſting habitation in purer ſkies, *in the new heaven and in the new earth, wherein righteouſneſs dwells.* I wiſh, friends, we may be effectually animated by the conſideration of theſe things : that, ſeeing every thing is uncertain, and that we may be deprived of the choiceſt of terreſtrial bleſſings in an unexpected hour, let us *ſeek a city that hath foundations, and*

lay

lay up for ourselves a good foundation against the time which is to come.

It is, indeed, to be acknowledged, with reverent gratitude and praise, that many are the bleſſings we have received in the courſe of God's providence ; and we ought to receive them in a humble becoming manner,—in a manner becoming dependent beings, who have nothing which they have not received, and to uſe, or apply, them to the purpoſe for which they were given. But we are not to reſt ſatisfied in thoſe enjoyments which are to be derived merely from an intercourſe with terreſtrial objects. *Ariſe, and go hence ; this is not thy reſt ! But there is a reſt prepared for the people of God ;* and that reſt is to be attained by a reverent attention to his commandments. This is the conſtant doctrine of the holy Scriptures, both in the old and in the new Teſtament : let us, therefore, ſtudy the will of heaven reſpecting us; and let it be our conſtant concern to recommend ourſelves to the Author of our being, by manifeſting

the

the love, we feel or poſſeſs for him, in a reverent attention to his ſtatutes and his commandments. Were our hearts thus diſ-poſed heaven-ward to ſeek the ſuperior good, we ſhould be able to join with the royal pſalmiſt in ſaying, *My ſoul thirſteth for God, for the living God!* Again, *As the hart panteth after the water-brooks, ſo panteth my ſoul after thee, O God!* A contempla-tion of the divine law, to thoſe who love it, would open a ſource of the moſt exalted pleaſure, and they would in-deed ſay with the pſalmiſt, *Thy ſtatutes are my ſongs in the houſe of my pilgrimage.* Now I underſtand, by *ſongs* in the text, that they were the chief, or principal, ob-jects of his affections; that they were in-ſcribed on the tablet of his heart, as well as written on the poſts of his doors. They were the ſubjects of his meditation when he lay down and when he roſe up.

May it pleaſe the Author of all good ſo to inſpire our hearts with a noble contempt of all ſenſual indulgences, as that we may

purſue

purfue thofe things which are moft excellent ; and, feeing the infufficiency of all
terreftrial fcenes to communicate to us permanent felicity, we may fet our affections
on things which are above, and, by a courfe
of practical virtue and obedience, lay up
for ourfelves treafure in heaven, where
the moth nor ruft cannot corrupt, nor
thieves break through, and fteal. Then
fhall we ultimately attain that reft which is
prepared for the people of God, in which
there is fulnefs of joy!

DISCOURSE

DISCOURSE V.

THERE is a paſſage of holy writ which hath engaged my ſerious meditation. You will find it, on ſacred record, in words to this purport :

If thine own heart condemn thee not, then haſt thou confidence towards God ; by which I have underſtood, thou haſt confidence, and a humble expectation of the divine bleſſing, and that thou ſhalt be accepted of the Judge of the whole earth in the day of judgement, the day of final deciſion.

The

The apoftle alfo fays, *But, if thine own heart condemn thee, remember that God is greater, and knoweth all things* ; by which I have underftood, that, if we ftand condemned at the tribunal of our own hearts, we fhall not be approved of him, who looketh not as man looketh, but looketh at the heart.

I conceive, however, that this paffage is not to be admitted without fome exception ; for, it is poffible that fome people may have digreffed fo widely from the paths of truth and virtue, and funk fo deeply into the loweft fpecies of fenfuality, as to have their underftandings clouded, and perceive not the propriety and the excellency of virtue. Their confciences are become *feared as with a hot iron*. Reiterated tranfgreffion of the divine law renders the heart, as it were, in fome degree, callous, and it lofes that delicate moral fenfibility diftinguifhed by the appellation of confcience. On the other hand, fome pious well-difpofed people, afflicted perhaps by fome fpecies of natural difeafe,

diſeaſe, have let in, and cheriſhed, ground-
leſs fears and apprehenſions, have thought
themſelves ſo morally depraved and pollu-
ted, that, though ſome of them ſeem to be
the beſt of mankind, we may have obſerved
them to have been brought to the confines
of the horrible pit of deſpair. Theſe may,
I think, be conſidered as exceptions to this
general rule of the apoſtle.

Now I conceive the apoſtle intended to
this purport ; that, whoever wiſhes to receive the beſt information reſpecting the
duties which he owes to his Maker and to
his fellow-creatures, and purſues thoſe
means of inſtruction which he apprehends
will be the moſt conducive to obtain it, and
who conforms his life, his manners, and his
converſation, agreeably to that knowledge
which he has received, as he will not be
condemned of his own heart, but have the
teſtimony of a *conſcience void of offence towards God and towards man*, ſo he will be
approved of his Maker, and approved of
the wiſe, the diſcerning, and the good, of
all

all ranks and denominations of men. On
the contrary, the man who wilfully acts a-
gainſt the ſober dictates of his judgement,
will of courſe (unleſs he becomes indeed a
reprobate) feel the teſtimony of his own
conſcience againſt him. Perhaps this moral ſenſibility may not always attend him.
In his convivial hours,—hours that are ſet
apart for the gratification of merely ſenſual
appetites, — hours that are paſſed in
unholy delights, in rioting and *drunkenneſs,
in chambering and wantonneſs,* he may not be
ſuſceptible of the impreſſions of conſcience;
yet, in the moments of his receſs, when he
retires from the pleaſing and deluſive ſcenes
of vanity, in the moments of cool reflection, he will feel the teſtimony of his own
conſcience, which may prompt him to act
in a manner ſimilar to that of our great
primogenitor, who, in the calm evening of
the day, remembered the tranſgreſſion of
the morn, felt the reproaches of his own
conſcience, and attempted to hide himſelf
from the all-penetrating eye of the Lord of
the

the univerfe. *Adam, where art thou ?* He
hid himfelf among the trees of the garden ; and thus it is with us, or has been,
more or lefs, with us all. We firft tranfgreffed, and then fought to hide our tranfgreffion ; for, it is my firm opinion, that,
if mankind were as heartily concerned to
reform their evil practices as they are to
conceal them, the work of reformation
would foon be more ftriking and apparent
amongft the feveral ranks and claffes of
mankind.

Whoever has the teftimony of his confcience againft him will have no folid
foundation of hope, or expectation, of being approved of him whofe laws he has
tranfgreffed, whofe ftatutes he has viola-
ted.

I wifh, my friends, we might be all fuit-
ably impreffed with the importance of this
fubject. It is of all others the moft interefting to us,—*a good confcience.*

But it is exceedingly to be regretted that
this fpecies of good, this fpecies of riches,

I   is

is too seldom the object of our pursuit. In this world, we are as a guest that tarrieth but for half an hour. In a short time, those who possess goodly inheritances must leave them to their children or heirs. Generation succeeds to generation very quickly. Were we, therefore, to possess all the riches of this world; were we to be made proprietors of the world itself, under the anticipation of that solemn period when we shall be about to quit this terrestrial sphere, what is it that a man would not *give in exchange for his soul !* What is it he would not part with, were it in the power of his disposal, for the testimony of a *good conscience*, to give him a humble confidence towards God, that the future state he is just entering upon shall be within the confines of the general assembly of the just and purified spirits, who, in the fruition of eternal joy, receive the *end of their faith*, even the *salvation of their souls !*

I beseech you, my friends, in the love of the gospel of Christ, that ye *walk wisely,*

that

that ye be *circumſpect*, that ye ſtudy, in the firſt place, your reſpective duties, that you be prompted by the pureſt and worthieſt motives to act agreeably with the information you have received, that ſo you may poſſeſs this ineſtimable bleſſing, a *good conſcience*, or a *conſcience void of offence both towards God and towards man.*

This is that ſpecies of treaſure which we are exhorted to *lay up for ourſelves in heaven, in bags that wax not old, where the moth and the ruſt cannot corrupt, nor thieves break through and ſteal.* This is the ſpecies of riches, and the only ſpecies of riches, which the craft and violence of others cannot wreſt from us; for, it is ſecured beyond the power of plunder: it is ſecured in a man's own heart, over which his neighbour can have no controul. But, whatever elſe he poſſeſſes, he may, in the courſe of divine providence, be ſtripped of. He may loſe his fair inheritance; it may be tranſlated to the hands of others by events which human wiſdom could not foreſee, nor hu-

man

man prudence prevent. He may be ſtripped of all his property, and be brought to
penury and want; but the teſtimony of a
good conſcience cannot be taken from a
man : it muſt be given away, — it muſt be
voluntarily parted with, by a tranſgreſſion
of thoſe dictates which may be called the
law of conſcience. Therefore let us lay up
for ourſelves a good foundation againſt the
time to come.

But I am aware of an objection which,
perhaps, may be made. It is this : the
excellency of a good conſcience is univerſal-
ly admitted ; but where is the man who
poſſeſſes this ineſtimable treaſure ? Where
is the man who can lay his hand upon his
heart, and ſay, that it *condemns him not ?*
Upon a review of the actions of his life,
and the influencing motives of his conduct,
where is the man who can lay his hand upon his heart, and pronounce himſelf imma-
culate?

I believe there is not ſuch a man exiſt-
ing; that is to ſay, a man that doth not ſin,

or

or hath not aforetime finned ; *for, all have finned, and fallen fhort of the glory of God,* and of courfe have forfeited thofe glorious privileges which were poffeffed by our primogenitors in their paradifiacal ftate, before they tranfgreffed the divine law. We have finned, and fallen fhort of the glory of God ; but we are abundantly inftructed, both in the old and new Teftament, that the Author of our being *willeth not the death of the finner,*— that he willeth not the deftruction of creatures which he hath formed capable of eternal life. He is not difpofed, at all events, to confign them to the realms of irremediable woe and mifery, but has manifefted himfelf towards his creatures in the character not only of a juft, but also of a merciful and gracious, being ; a being who compaffionates the infirmities, the weakneffes, and wanderings, of his creatures, and who hath provided a means for the redemption of mankind from fin, and, of courfe, from mifery : — that means is Jefus Chrift, the mediator of the

I 3

new covenant, the high-prieft of the Chriftian difpenfation, conftituted, not after the
law of a carnal commandment, but after
the power of an endlefs life, who remain-
eth a prieft for ever. *It is a faithful faying,
and it is worthy of all acceptation, that Jefus
Chrift came into the world to fave finners;* not
to fave them in their fins, but to fave them
from their fins, to cleanfe them from all
unrighteoufnefs, to reftore unto his creatures the glorious liberty of the fons of
God, and, of confequence, a good confcience : *Wherefore,* fays the apoftle, *we
truft we have a good confcience.*

This is the great and glorious purpofe of
the manifeftation of the Son of God, that,
notwithftanding we have finned, and fallen
fhort of his glory; that we all, as fheep,
have gone aftray from the fheepfold, and
have wandered in the wildernefs of this
world, yet, if *we confefs our fins, God is
faithful and juft to forgive us our fins, and to
cleanfe us from all unrighteoufnefs;* by which
I underftand, that the office of the mediator

tor is not only to be the means of the remiffion of fins that are paft, through the forbearance of God, but that his office alfo is
to cleanfe and fanctify the penitent foul,—to
cleanfe it from all unrighteoufnefs, and, of
courfe, it will have a good confcience, and
have confidence towards God. Now thefe
are general propofitions, to which we all
accede. Offers of mercy are held out to us
through Jefus Chrift our Lord, and our
confciences will moft certainly condemn us
unlefs we attempt to apply thofe offers, to
apply thofe healing qualities, unto ourfelves. The teftimony of our confciences
will ftand againft us if we neglect this great
falvation, which is offered to us through
Jefus Chrift our Lord. I befeech you,
therefore, by the mercies of God, (than
which there is nothing, perhaps, more
likely to influence the fenfible and judicious
part of mankind, who open their eyes, and
view the vaft extent of the divine empire;—
who contemplate the phænomena of nature, and the feveral means that the Au-

thor

thor of nature has taken for the conferva-
tion of all the fpecies of his creatures, *I
befeech you, therefore, brethren, by the mercies of God,) that you prefent your bodies a
living facrifice, holy and acceptable to God,
which is our reafonable fervice.* But there is
no facrifice that can be offered upon the altar of God, there is no prayer whatever
which claims the notice of the Lord God
of Sabaoth, which is not the offspring of
a humble, of a devoted, heart, fenfible of
its weaknefs, fenfible of its unworthinefs,
and of a purity of intention to apply thofe
means for its redemption, and to purfue
thofe methods, for the future, which fhall
receive the teftimony of confcience, and
the recompence of the juft at the laft day.

Let it, then, be the firft object of our
attention to feek a good confcience. Let
us think every thing elfe but as drofs and
as dung. Every acquifition we may make
within the compafs of the creation, bears
no proportion to the bleffing of a good
confcience; for, poffeffing this, a man has

peace

peace at home. Whatever tumults may a-
rife, whatever winds may blow, whatever
afflictions may furround him, thefe will but
play round his head ; they cannot reach his
heart ; for, *the good man fhall be fatisfied from
himfelf.* He will have a fource of fatisfaction in himfelf, which will diffipate every
gloom,—a fatisfaction the fenfual are ftrangers to. He will look beyond the confines
of time, and expect a habitation *in the new
heavens and the new earth, wherein righteoufnefs
dwells.* Though men fhould look upon his
life to be without ufe, and his end without
honour, yet he will be approved of God,
and the lot of his inheritance will be with
the faints. But, if a man does not poffefs
the teftimony of his own confcience, he
cannot be happy in any circumftance of
life. Wherever he goes, his confcience
will attend him ; and, even in the houfe of
banqueting, he will fometimes, as it were,
fee a hand-writing on the wall, *Thou art
weighed in the balance, and found wanting.*
If he come to the greateft honour and
preferment,

preferment, ftill he will be like Cain ; and, having a bad confcience, may be doomed to compafs the earth without being able to make a happy fettlement in any part of it. He has no peace in himfelf : he is feeking for that without, which muft be found (if ever it be found) within, him ; for, if a man be completely fatisfied, it muft be from himfelf : (it muft not, however, be confidered as the effect of his moral con-duct, apart from Jefus Chrift ; it muft pro-ceed from that pure ftate which is termed, in the facred writings, *regeneration.)* His affections muft be tranflated from creature-ly objects to the Creator. They muft be fet, not on things beneath, but on things which are above, and then it will become the object of his purfuit, to lay up trea-fure in heaven ; and, where the treafure is, there will the heart be alfo.

But, let it not be imagined that that is peculiar to an inhabitant above the ftars. Let it not be imagined that he muft afcend to the heights above to feel the joys of the

com-

community, or fociety, of purified fpirits;
for, the juft upon earth, and the glorified in
heaven, participate of the fame eternal
Fountain of mercy, goodnefs, and truth:
they are replenifhed at the fame immortal
Fountain of mercy and goodnefs; — a
Fountain, that can never be drawn dry, —a
Fountain, at which the righteous of all denominations have drunk. They have been
refrefhed with thofe ftreams which inter-
fect this vale of tears; and, as they have
paffed along, they have experienced a growth
in grace, and in the faving knowledge of
the Lord Jefus Chrift. They have enjoyed
a foretafte of that fpecies of felicity *which
eye hath not feen, ear hath not heard, nor hath
it entered into the heart of man*, unregenerate
man, *to conceive*. This is written for all
that fhall be joined to the fociety of the
juft; not to any tribe or nation in particular, but to people of all names and tongues
that *fear God and work righteousfnefs*, whofe
hearts

hearts condemn them not, who poſſeſs the teſtimony of a good conſcience.

We are told, that the kingdom of heaven is within us ; and our Lord, forewarning his diſciples concerning the deceivers of the enſuing times, who ſhould ſay, *Lo, here is Chriſt*, and *lo, there is Chriſt !* cautions them, ſaying, go not forth after them : the kingdom of heaven, ſays he, is within you. And, in another place, it is defined to be righteouſneſs, peace, and joy, in the Holy Ghoſt. Then, wherever there is the beauty of righteouſneſs, wherever there is that moral rectitude which is conſonant to the law of God, there is the kingdom of heaven,— there is the temple of the Holy Ghoſt ; and, thus ſanctified in the name of the Moſt High, the veſſel bears the inſcription of *Holineſs to the Lord! The kingdom of heaven is within you.* Let us be concerned to experience that rectitude of heart, that converſion of ſoul, which will qualify us to enjoy the incomes of the Holy Spirit, — that

will

will qualify us to have *communion with the Father, and with his Son Jesus Christ.*

I commend thefe obfervations to your ferious confideration, befeeching you, my friends, let it be the firft object of your ftudy to attain and keep a good confcience. If we are confcious of having finned, let us implore the interpofition of the divine mercy; let us be proftrate at the footftool of the throne of divine grace; let us attempt to feel thofe affections, thofe penitential affections, that will prompt us to enter into the temple of the Moft High, in a difpofition of mind fuitable to the occafion, and fimilar to that of the poor publican. We have nothing that we can boaft of. Indeed, the moft exalted among men have nothing to boaft of in the fight of God. After we have difcharged our obligations, we are *unprofitable fervants.* We are unprofitable to him, and have nothing to claim upon the fcore of merit, becaufe we have done nothing but what was our duty.

Let

Let us, impreffed, therefore, with thefe motives, *lay afide every weight, and the fin which doth fo eafily befet us, and run with patience the race that is fet before us.* Let it be *the juft man's path,* to which the eye of our mind may be allured, and our feet be turned, which is *as a fhining light, that fhineth more and more unto the perfect day.* That, as we pafs along, and as we grow in years, we may grow in grace, we may grow in favour with the common Father of us all: that, when our natural fun may be on the decline, and nearly fet, whether we are in the meridian or evening of old age, we may have a profpect of immortality; and, having our fun fet in an unclouded horizon, it may be to us the glorious prefage of an eternal fair day.

I commend us to God, and to a humble attention to the manifeftation of that Spirit *which he hath given to every man to profit withal,* and which is adapted to the proper information of our judgements, to ftrengthen our virtuous refolutions, to guide us by its counfels through the wildernefs of this world,

world, and eſtabliſh us in the realms of glory, where, *with ſaints and angels, and the ſpirits of juſt men made perfeƐt*, we may celebrate the praiſes of the Author of our being. Thus, if we aƐt wiſely, and wiſh to poſſeſs a good conſcience, we ſhall be tranſlated to that ſphere where *the wiſe ſhall ſhine as the brightneſs of the firmament, and they, that turn many unto righteouſneſs, as the ſtars, for ever and ever !*

PRAYER

PRAYER

AT THE

CONCLUSION of the MEETING.

MOST gracious Creator, it is of thine infinite mercy that thou deigneſt to hear our prayers, or takeſt the leaſt favourable notice of us ; for, we have all, as loſt ſheep, gone aſtray : we have ſinned, and forſaken thy ſtatutes, as our fathers have done. We are, therefore, unworthy of the leaſt of thy mercies and grace, yet thou art pleaſed to encourage us to approach thy ſacred altar, to hum-

ble

ble ourfelves before thee, and to offer up our fupplications unto thee, the common Father of us all. Though heaven be thy throne, and the earth thy footftool, yet thou not only heareft, but hearkeneft, to the voice of the prayer of thy creatures. The prayer of any, and every, penitent foul penetrates the heavens, and reaches thee. O moft holy and merciful God, imprefs us, at this feafon, we humbly befeech thee, with fuitable affections of foul to enter into thy houfe of prayer, and lift up our hearts with our hands to the habitation of thy holinefs, fenfible, moft holy God, of thy infinite purity, and of that impurity which we have contracted by the tranfgreffion of thy law. We implore the extenfion of thy mercy, through Jefus Chrift, for the remiffion of fins that are paft, and that thou wouldft be pleafed effectually to cleanfe and fanctify us, through the operation of thy holy Spirit, before we fhall go hence, and be no more feen; that, having a hope of immortality, we may be enabled,

K   by

by the aid of thy Spirit, to pafs the time
of our fojourning here in fear, and, being
concerned above all things to retain in our
poffeffion the teftimony of a good confcience, we may be accepted of the Judge of
the whole earth at the laft day; that, in
a folemn view of thy greatnefs, our fouls
may be humbled, that, under the influence
of thy holy Spirit, we may offer up to thee
the incenfe of thankfgiving and praife, afcribing to thee might, majefty, and glory,
dominion, and every other excellent attribute with which thou art furrounded, now
and for evermore. Amen.

DISCOURSE

DISCOURSE VI.

*WITHOUT Faith it is impossible to
please God; for, he that cometh unto
God must believe that he is, and that he is a
rewarder of them that diligently seek him.*

The revival of this passage of holy writ,
in my remembrance, hath been the means
of exciting and fixing my attention upon
the subject of faith.

It cannot, I conceive, have escaped the
observation of any person, who is arrived
at years of understanding, and is conversant

with

with the holy Scriptures, that the fame
word *faith* hath divers acceptations : that,
in fome places, it intends not only a belief
in the exiftence of an infinitely wife, powerful, and intelligent, Being, who is a rewarder of them who diligently feek him;
but alfo an affiance, or truft, in feafons of
adverfity and probation, in that Being who
has all power in heaven and earth, whofe
power is uncontroulable, who doeth whatfoever pleafeth him in the armies of heaven
and amongft the inhabitants of the earth.
— The word *faith* is alfo ufed to diftinguifh
between the different difpenfations; to
point out the glorious difpenfation of the
Gofpel of Chrift, which is called the *law
of faith*, and to contradiftinguifh it from
the Mofaic difpenfation, which is called
the *law of works*; and I conceive, that,
wherever any of the writers of the New
Teftament fpeak of the infignificancy of
works, with refpect to the rendering a man
acceptable to the Author of his being, the
works of the law, or, to ufe the apoftle's
expreffion,

expreffion, the deeds of the law, by which no flefh living can be juftified, are intended. The rituals of the legal difpenfation are not of a nature to be trufted in. Our Saviour, in his perfon, fulfilled the obligation of that law, and was the end of that law for righteoufnefs fake. It is therefore written, that he has taken away the hand-writing of ordinances, and nailed them to his crofs, which muft refpect the rituals of the Mofaic difpenfation.

Some people, whom I need not uncharitably cenfure, have, I conceive, entertained a miftaken notion refpecting the nature of that faith which is effectual, through Chrift, to the falvation of the foul. They have apprehended, that a belief in the exiftence of the fupreme Being, and a belief in Jefus Chrift, whom God has fent, is of itfelf fufficient, and, unto whomfoever this faith is given, they are to be deemed of the number of the chofen few, whom God predeftinated from everlafting unto eternal life; and that this faith, apart from the

K 3   confideration

confideration of works, is fufficient unto
falvation :——but to me it appears, on the
moft ferious inveftigation of the Holy
Scriptures, that, as without faith it is im-
poffible to pleafe God, fo with faith it is
poffible to difpleafe him. This is a propofition which I conceive might be proved
from divers parts of the New Teftament
efpecially; more particularly where we are
told of people, who, after they knew God,
(it implies that he was manifefted unto
them,) after they knew God, they glorified
him not as God, but became vain in their
imaginations, and their foolifh hearts became darkened. They glorified him not as
God, that is, they brought not forth thofe
good fruits, by which it is faid, that our
Father who is in heaven is glorified; for,
herein, fays our Lord, is my heavenly Father glorified, in that ye bring forth much
fruit; by which undoubtedly the fruits of
the Spirit are intended, joy, peace, love,
long-fuffering, gentlenefs, goodnefs, and
faith. — It is poffible that a man may be
convinced

convinced with respect to the truth of certain propositions received upon the authority, the divine authority, of him who pro-
poses them, and yet may act in direct con-
tradiction to the obligation of those laws.
Now we are in divers places instructed
respecting the essentiality of faith; that it
is a lively operating principle of the judgement, which hath a moral influence upon
a man's actions; not a mere barren speculative faith; but a faith that worketh by
love, — to what? to the purifying of the
conscience from all dead works, to serve the
living God, not in the oldness of the letter, but in the newness of the Spirit, and
with life; and, left the primitive Christians
should entertain a mistaken notion of the
efficacy of faith in the abstract, and should
rest their hopes of salvation upon their
subscription to certain articles of faith,
though those articles be founded upon the
basis of immutable truth, the apostle takes
occasion to instruct them that faith without
works is dead: Thinkest thou, O vain

K 4   man,

man, that faith can fave thee? the very devils (fays he) believe, the very devils believe, and they alfo tremble; for, as the
body without the foul is dead, fo faith
without works is dead alfo; and he propofed a teft, a teft of faving faith, which is
eafy and obvious, and ought to be more
confulted than it is by the feveral claffes
and focieties of religious profeffors: Shew
me (fays he) thy faith without thy works,
and I will fhew thee my faith by my works,
for, the tree is to be denominated by its fruit:
by their fruits you fhall know them. The
true believer is diftinguifhed from the practical infidel by his fruits; he brings forth
fruits meet for repentance; he adds, to his
faith, virtue; to virtue, knowledge; to
knowledge, temperance; to temperance,
brotherly kindnefs; and to brotherly kindnefs, charity: and, if thefe things (fays
the apoftle) be in you, and abound, they
fhall make you that ye fhall neither be barren nor unfruitful in the faving knowledge
of our Lord Jefus Chrift. *Shew me thy*
faith

faith without thy works; a man may have
the cleareft conception of truth without
reducing this theory into practice in his
own perfon. To apprehend the right is
one thing; to conform ourfelves to the rule
of right, in our lives and in our manners,
is another thing; therefore it feems, to me,
beyond the leaft degree of doubt, that
fomething more than a fpeculative belief,
or a faith in certain propofitions, is neceffary to render us acceptable to the fupreme
Being, and to qualify us for an inheritance
among the faints in light, to be heirs of
God, and co-heirs with Chrift. And I
wifh, as it is a matter of infinite importance to us all, that we, agreeable to the
advice of the apoftle to the members of the
primitive church, might examine ourfelves
whether we are in the faith : *Prove your own
felves*; *know ye not yourfelves how that Jefus
Chrift is in you unlefs ye be reprobates?* Let
us not content ourfelves, that we are the
defcendants of reputed Chriftian parents,
that we have been made acquainted with the

contents

contents of the facred hiftory of the old and of the new Teftament; let us not reft fatisfied merely with a profeffion of the Chriftian religion in theory, but let us alfo be concerned to act confiftently with the nature and obligation of that holy religion which Jefus Chrift was fent of the Father to promote among the fons and daughters of men.

The obligations and the Chriftian duties enjoined in the New Teftament are adapted at once to better our condition in this world, to make us happier in our fhort pilgrimage through it, and alfo to fecure to us ever-lafting felicity in the world which is to come. Let us not forget that our Lord fays, *It is not every one that fays, Lord, Lord, that fhall enter into the kingdom of heaven; but he that doeth the will of my Father, who is in heaven.* And again our Lord inftructs us thus: *If thou wilt enter into life, keep the commandments.*

By good works, I mean a conformity of the will and of the powers of the mind to that

that law or rule of action, which is of God given unto man, to illuminate his paths in this world, and guide him by his counfel to the participation of the realms of eternal glory; and as the power of obedience is derived from him, the Author of all that is excellent and good, as he is the giver of every good and perfect gift, fo that power is given unto us, through Jefus Chrift, by which we are capable of difcharging our feveral obligations. I fay, it being the gift of God, and not inherent in the creature, we afcribe all unto him, who is the efficient caufe of all holinefs and virtue in every part of his vaftly-extended empire ; for, it is God that works in us to do according to his own good pleafure, which pleafure is, that we fhould walk circumfpectly, not as fools, but as wife, redeeming the time, feeing that the days are evil ; that we (to ufe the language of the apoftle) fhould be *care-ful to maintain good works, which are good and profitable unto men.* I pretend not that they are profitable unto God; but they are

profitable

profitable unto men ; and godlinefs (which implies the obligation of practical duties, as well as ftedfaftly believing) is profitable for all things, having the promife of the life that now is, and alfo of that which is to come ; but I may fay, in the language of one formerly on this fubject, with refpect to the fupreme Being, who is perfect, felf-fufficient, and can receive nothing from his creatures, to whom he has communicated every thing, *If thou be righteous, what givest thou him, or what receiveth he of thine hand ? thy wickednefs may hurt a man as thou art, and thy righteoufnefs may profit the children of men.* It is for this purpofe, this noble, this difinterefted, purpofe, that the Almighty has eftablifhed a law to his creatures, not for his own profit, but for theirs. Hence it is faid, that the fabbath was made for man, and not man for the fabbath.

In the wifdom and fupreme goodnefs of the Creator, the obligation of Chriftian duties, in all circumftances, is adapted to the nature and capacity of his creatures, to promote

promote righteoufnefs through all the ranks and claffes of fociety; and, were but our obedience proportionate to our knowledge, did we act confiftently with the dictates of our judgement and the dictates of our faith, we might hope to fee the revival of that ftate, *when the morning ftars fang together, and the fons of God fhouted for joy.*

Examine yourfelves, whether you are in the faith; for, we are abundantly in-ftructed, as I have already obferved, that the faith that is faving is productive of good works; and it is the beft and fureft teft whereby to try whether a man has a faving or only a fpeculative faith, as the tree is to be known by his fruits; for men do not ga-ther grapes of thorns, nor figs of thiftles. Therefore that profeffor of the Chriftian religion, the tenor of whofe actions gives the lie to his profeffion; that profeffor gives a manifeftation that he has only a traditional religion, a traditional zeal, and a traditional faith, like the people of the Jews, who expreffed a veneration for the

temple

temple of the moft high God, and the rituals of thc legal difpenfation, and cried,
*The temple of the Lord, the temple of the
Lord, the temple of the Lord, are thefe.* But
the prophet faid, *Truft ye not in lying words,
faying, the temple of the Lord, the temple of
the Lord; but amend your ways and your
doings.*

Many and glorious are the privileges that
are to be enjoyed by the believer, fuch a
perfon as I have attempted to defcribe, who
not only believes in the infinitely fupreme
and powerful Being; in the manifeftation
of his Son; in the hiftory of his life, of
his death, of his refurrection, of his afcenfion into glory, and in the principles
and doctrines which he propagated; but
who manifefts that he has a faith that
worketh by love, the tendency of which is
to purify the confcience from dead works,
to cleanfe it from all unrighteoufnefs, that
the foul of man may become the temple of
the Holy Ghoft. —— Great and glorious
privileges are to be enjoyed by thofe few,

by

by thofe of whatever religious fociety, who
are partakers of true faving faith ; for, it is
worthy of being noted, that the Author of
the Chriftian religion is of no party, but
the friend of all; that his grace, like the
rays of the fun, is extended to all, from
fea to fea, and from the rivers unto the
ends of the earth; infomuch that we are
told in the Scriptures, that the Gofpel is
preached in every creature under heaven;
that all have heard, though all have not
obeyed.

Thofe, that are true believers, are of
that ftock and family unto whom it was
faid, *Fear not, little flock; it is your Father's good pleafure to give you the kingdom.
I am,* fays our Lord, *the refurrection and the
life; he, that believeth in me, though he were dead,
yet fhall he live, and he, that liveth and believeth
on me, fhall never die.* We muft note, on this
paffage, that here, as well as in many other
places in the New and in the Old Teftament, we are not to take the fenfe of the
Holy Ghoft in a merely literal acceptation,

becaufe

becaufe this would be to admit of a doctrine contrary to the nature of things, and
contrary to fact. For inftance, the dead
are incapable of belief or difbelief, literally
fpeaking; they are filent in the grave, and
therefore are incapable of faith; it therefore muft intend thofe who are dead in trefpaffes and fins, aliens to the common-
wealth of Ifrael, ftrangers to the promifes
of the Gofpel of Chrift, loft and funk in a
fea of fenfuality: thefe are they to whom
the voice of the Son of God is extended,
and thofe that hear may yet live; they may
awake unto righteoufnefs, and fin not.
Whofoever, therefore, believes in me, that is
to fay, who receives me in the name of
him that fent me, who embraces the doctrine I preach, who fubmits to the influence of the Holy Spirit given to them
of me from the Father, thofe who become
obedient to the word that I teach, *though he
were dead, yet fhall he live*; he fhall be
brought to live a life of righteoufnefs, he
will bring forth the fruit of righteoufnefs,
and

and the work of righteoufnefs fhall be peace,
and the effect fhall be quietnefs and affu-
rance for ever : and *he, that liveth and believeth in me, fhall never die :* this is not,
and cannot, be true in a literal fenfe ; for,
we fee that death happens to the righteous
and to the wicked, to him that facrificeth
as well as to him that facrificeth not ; it
muft therefore be intended in a fpiritual
fenfe ; he, that liveth and believeth in me,
fhall never die, fhall never participate of
that future woe and mifery defcribed under
the character of the fecond death ; he fhall
be redeemed from the bondage of fpiritual
death, and reftored into *the glorious liberty of
the fons of God*; he fhall live a life of righteoufnefs here, he fhall enjoy fpiritual communion with the Author of his being, he
fhall have fellowfhip with the Father, and
with his Son Jefus Chrift ; and, after the
diffolution of this body, he fhall be ufhered
into the realms of eternal life, he fhall be
united with the affembly of the juft, the

L   church

church of the firſt-born triumphant in glory.

Examine yourſelves, whether you are in the faith. Let not us, as a people, any more than others, preſume upon the pro-feſſion of a belief in certain Scripture-doctrines, or in the profeſſion of certain ar-ticles of faith ; but let us always remem-ber, that, if ever we are capable of ſuſ-taining the dignity of ſaints in heaven, we muſt live the life of the juſt upon the earth ; we muſt purſue the juſt man's way, *which is as a ſhining light, which ſhineth more and more unto the perfect day.*

The obligation to practical religion, which I have attempted to impreſs upon the minds of this auditory, is yet more ſtrong-ly enforced, by the Author of the Chriſ-tian diſpenſation, at the cloſe of that moſt excellent ſermon which he preached on the mount. After having opened the heavenly treaſures of doctrine, he concludes with ſaying, *If any man heareth theſe ſayings of mine, and doeth them not, he ſhall be likened to a fooliſh a foolish man, who built his house upon the sand.* This is the cafe of the merely nominal Chriftian; he heareth, believeth, or affenteth to the doctrines of the Gofpel of Chrift; *if any man heareth thefe fayings of mine, and doeth them not, he fhall be likened unto a foolifh man, who built his houfe upon the sand; and the rain defcended, and the floods came, and the winds blew, and beat upon that houfe, and it fell, and great was the fall thereof.* On the contrary, he defcribes the man who indeed poffeffes faving faith, the faith of our Lord Jefus Chrift; the man who will receive, at the clofe of his labours beneath the fun, the end of his faith, even the everlafting falvation of his foul: *if any man heareth thefe fayings of mine, and doeth them, I will liken him unto a wife man, who built his houfe upon a rock; and the rain defcended, and the floods came, and the winds blew, and beat upon that houfe, and it fell not, becaufe it was* fixed upon an immutable bafis; for, it was *founded upon a rock.* This man builds upon that rock,

againſt

againſt which the gates of hell can never prevail.

God Almighty grant, that of his infinite mercy and goodneſs we may examine the foundation we are building upon, whether the hopes and expectations we have, of being ſaved with an everlaſting ſalvation, be founded upon a ſpeculative faith, or upon ſuch a belief in the ſupreme Being, and in his Son, as may conform us in heart to that law, that rule of action, which the Author of univerſal nature has diſpenſed and given to all the claſſes of intelligent beings.

Examine yourſelves, whether you are in the faith; prove your own ſelves; know ye not your own ſelves, how that Jeſus Chriſt is in you, except you be reprobates? The manifeſtation of the grace of God here intended is in every man, and its deſign is to inſtruct him in that which is right, and to ſtrengthen him in the performance of every virtue. This is the purpoſe of the manifeſtation of that grace which bringeth ſalvation, and which

which is given unto all men, not to a few,
to the exclufion of the reft; but, through
the infinite mercy of the fupreme Being, it
is given to all men, and under all defcrip-
tions, teaching us that, *denying ungodlinefs
and worldly lufts, we fhould live foberly, righteoufly, and godly, in this prefent world, looking for the bleffed hope and the glorious appearing of the great God and of our Saviour
Jefus Chrift, who hath given himfelf for us,
that he might redeem us from all iniquity, and
purify to himfelf a peculiar people zealous of
good works.* — Let us not therefore neglect
our own mercies, by neglecting that falvation which is offered to us through Jefus
Chrift our Lord. Let us be ferious, let us
be inquifitive, upon a matter of fo great
importance as that upon which our happinefs in the world of fpirits moft certainly
depends; let us not content ourfelves with
the form and fhow of godlinefs, while we
are deftitute of its life, and of its power
and heavenly virtue. May our hearts enter
into the nature and fpirit of true Chriftian

L 3   faith,

faith, that by this means we may have accefs to the Father through the Son, and
that in thefe our religious and folemn affemblies we may poffefs that faith by which
Abel offered to God a more excellent facrifice than Cain; with that faith let us draw
near to the temple of the moft high, let us
approach to that altar to which none that
ferve the tabernacle can pretend; let us approach the Author of our being and of all
our mercies, that we may be difpofed by
him, the preparer of the heart, to receive
the falutary influences of the Holy Ghoft,
and that we may feel ourfelves under the
defcription of thofe, mentioned in the Old
Teftament, who wait upon the name of
the moft high: though *the youth may faint,
and though the young men may utterly fall,
yet they that wait upon the Lord fhall renew
their ftrength, they fhall mount up with wings
as eagles, they fhall run and not be weary,
they fhall walk and not faint.*

To conclude, as my mind feems to be
difburdened from that which appeared to be
my

my duty, and which I have been perform-
ing, I truft in the ability that God giveth,
without any kind of premeditation, under
the influence of that celeftial charity, which
breathes glory to God in the higheft, on
earth peace, and good will towards men;
under that influence, again I would enjoin
the exhortation of the apoftle : *Examine
yourfelves, whether you are in the faith; prove
your own felves ; know ye not your own felves,
how that Jefus Chrift is in you, except you be
reprobates?*

L 4   PRAYER

PRAYER

AT THE

CONCLUSION of the MEETING.

MOST gracious God, the father and fountain of all our mercies, look down from heaven, the habitation of thy holiness, upon us, thy poor unworthy creatures, and imprefs us with a juſt ſenſe of what we are, and alſo of what thou wouldſt have us to be; that, ſeeing ourſelves as we are ſeen of thee, we may abhor ourſelves in duſt and aſhes, and feel all that penitential contrition that is neceſſary

to

to render us the objects of thy mercy; that,
on a review of our paſt lives, we may ſee,
and ſincerely repent of, the tranſgreſſions
we have committed; and, under the influence of thine Holy Spirit, we may re-
ſolve, in the future ſteps of our ſhort pilgrimage, to correct the errors of thoſe that
are irrecoverably paſt. O Lord, enable us
to apply the means of ſalvation, which
thou art granting unto us through Jeſus
Chriſt our Lord, that we may receive in
meekneſs the ingrafted word which is able
to ſave our ſouls. O Lord, enlighten our
eyes to ſee, and inſpire our hearts to perform, thoſe things which make for our
peace, thoſe duties which thou haſt enjoined unto us of indiſpenſable obligation. —
Moſt gracious Father, thou knoweſt the
temptations with which we are beſet; thou
knoweſt the weakneſs of our natural powers,
and the ſtrength of thoſe temptations
which aſſail us. Send us, therefore, help
from thy ſanctuary; ſtrengthen us, O
Lord, and impart vigour to every virtuous
reſolution,

refolution, that we may be enabled to lay afide every weight and burthen, and the fin that does moft eafily befet us, and run with patience the race that is fet before us, in humble faith and confidence in thee, the Creator, the Protector, and the Preferver, of men; that, through whatever fcene it may be our lot to pafs, we may feel the fupport of thine everlafting arm, that, when we pafs through the valley of the fhadow of death, we may fear no evil, and, whenever it fhall pleafe thee to fummon us hence, it may be to join the general affembly and church of the firft-born, where, with faints and angels, and with the fpirits of juft men made perfect, we may ever live to praife thy great and excellent name, to afcribe to thee the greatnefs, dominion, and glory, which belong unto thee, not only now, but henceforth and for evermore. Amen.

DISCOURSE

DISCOURSE VII.

AN apoftle, writing to one of the primitive churches, addreffed them in
this manner or to this purport: *Quench not
the Spirit, defpife not prophefying; prove all
things, and hold faft that which is good.*

The writings both of the Old and the
New Teftament abundantly teftify, that
God doth not only reveal himfelf unto his
rational creatures in the volume of his
works, or the book of nature, in which the
attributes, particularly of power and of
intelligence, are eminently difplayed, but
that he alfo reveals himfelf unto his rational

tional creatures immediately by his Spirit, which I conceive to be the grand and primary rule or law of action to all ranks and classes of intelligent creatures, and that all other modes of the manifestation of his will are secondary, and subservient to the grand design or purpose thereof.

There is a spirit in man, (a rational capacity, by which he is eminently distinguished from the beasts of the field and the fowls of heaven,) *and the inspiration of the Almighty giveth him an understanding.* It is very observable, that one of the chosen leaders of the people of Israel, after having solemnly, by way of commemoration, recounted the signal interpositions of divine Power, in the emancipation of that people from under the tyranny of Pharaoh, as one instance of the divine goodness, he saith, *he gave us also his good Spirit to instruct us.* This manifestation of himself by his Spirit, though extraordinarily dispensed to many of the prophets, was more or less the privilege of every individual; and we find

find the royal pfalmift frequently alluding to this principle, and rejoicing therein: *The law,* fays he, *of the Lord, is perfect, converting the foul; the teftimony of the Lord is fure, making wife the fimple.* The law, which he in this place intended, I conceive to be that law of the fpirit of life in Chrift Jefus, which fets us free from the law of fin and death. — A manifeftation hereof was given even under the former difpenfation of Mofes; it was the conductor of that people, it was the fource of their greateft confolation; for, they all *drank of that rock that followed them; and that rock,* faith the apoftle, *was Chrift. The law of the Lord,* fays he, *is perfect;* by which he could not intend the law of rituals peculiar to that difpenfation, or the facrificial rites of the Jewifh inftitution; *for, the law,* fays the apoftle, *made nothing perfect.* Again he inftructeth us, that it made not perfect, as appertaining to the confcience: it is not the blood of bulls or of goats, or the afhes of an heifer, fprinkling the unclean, that

could

could fanctify to the purifying of the confcience; for, *the law made nothing perfect,
but the bringing in of a better hope did,* which
hope is Chrift.

That he (to wit, David) intended the primary divine law manifefted by the Spirit of
God unto his creatures, is evident from divers other places.— *I delight,* fays he, *in the
law of the Lord;* and again, *bleffed is the
man whofe delight is in the law of the Lord,
and in his law doth meditate day and night; he
fhall be as a tree that is planted by the rivers of
waters.* And, that his chief felicity de-
pended on an immediate union or communion with the God of Ifrael, is very evident from that place, where, under the
preffure of his infirmities, and confcious
of the want of fuperior aid, he breaks
forth in this manner: *My foul thirfteth for
God, yea, for the living God;* again, *as the
hart panteth after the water-brooks, fo
panteth my foul after thee, O God.*

Many other paffages might be produced,
from the writings even of the Old Teftament,

ment, while the Jewish tabernacle was yet remaining : but it is more, still more, abundantly testified by our Saviour and by his apostles. *The manifestation of the Spirit is given to every man to profit withal.* — This is that principle of intelligence given us in Jesus Christ, or through Jesus Christ, our Lord, which the apostle intended when he said, *quench not the Spirit*; which must certainly mean the inward manifestation of the Deity to the soul, that grace, a measure whereof is given to every man to profit withal; and, that it could not mean any written manifestation of himself, or the Scriptures, which some have conceived was intended by the Spirit, (who allege, that the Spirit, or the will, of God being revealed unto holy men immediately, was mediately communicated, through the instrumentality of the Scriptures, to the rest of mankind,) is very evident ; for, the canon of the New Testament was not not made up till some hundreds of years after the writing of this Epistle ; nor doth it appear, that
any

any epiftles or writings of the evangelifts were collected or completed even during the lives of the apoftles. The New Teftament, therefore, as a book, did not exift; but the apoftle alludes to fomething that had been received, which I take to be *the mani-feftation of the Spirit, that is given to every man to profit withal.*

This principle of intelligence, this ma-nifeftation of the divine will, its effects, its properties, and its influence upon the human foul, is fet forth under various figu-rative modes of expreffion. It is fometimes compared unto fire. As it is the property of fire to purify metal and feparate hetero-geneous matter, fo the Spirit of God, operating on the foul, will thoroughly *purge away its drofs and take away all its tin*; cleanfe the foul from all unrighteoufnefs, and of courfe make it a fit habitation of God through the Spirit.— Is not my word, faith the Lord, as a fire? as a fire to con-fume and deftroy that part in man which is at enmity with that which is good ? — and

therefore

therefore the office of the high prieft of this difpenfation is fet forth, under the fame figurative mode of expreffion, by him who was the forerunner of Chrift, who was the voice of one crying in the wildernefs, *prepare ye the way of the Lord, make his path ftrait.* He baptized the people, as he faid, indeed, with water, unto repentance ; but, when he fpeaks of the miniftration of Jefus, which was to fucceed his, he faith : *He, that cometh after me, is mightier than I; whofe fhoe-latchet I am not worthy to loofe ; he fhall baptize you with fire.* Now it cannot be conceived that the material element of fire is intended, which would deftroy men's bodies ; for, Jefus Chrift came not to deftroy men's lives, but to fave them. *He fhall baptize you with the Holy Ghoft and with fire ; whofe fan is in his hand, and he will thoroughly purge his floor, gather his wheat into his garner, and the chaff he will burn up with unquenchable fire.* This Scripture I adduce to fhew that the effects of the Holy Spirit upon the rational foul, the foul that

M   is

is depraved by the tranfgreffion of the divine law, and has contracted the defilement of fin, is analogous to the operation of that element, that is adapted to purify and refine material bodies. Thus it is faid, that a man, fanctified by the influence thereof, fhall become as pure as gold, yea, more pure than the golden wedge of Ophir. This I take to be the one effential baptifm, the baptifm of the Holy Ghoft, which cleanfeth men from all unrighteoufnefs, and which is neceffary to conftitute us the proper object of *that inheritance which is incorruptible and undefiled, and that fadeth not away.* For, the baptifm that now faves is not an elementary baptifm; the baptifm which now faves is not the putting away the filth of the flefh, than which nothing could be more eafy for a man to effectuate; but, it is that which gives the anfwer of a good confcience towards God, by the refurrection of Jefus Chrift, who hath faid, *I am the refurrection and the life; he, who believeth on me, though he were dead, yet fhall*

he

he live; and he, who liveth and believeth on me, fhall never die.

Quench not the Spirit. The fimile, or figure, is very well maintained; for, as the property of the Holy Spirit is fet forth under the metaphorical language of fire, fo that, which has a tendency to damp its ge-nerous ardour, or prevent its influence, is compared to water. In a moral fenfe, whatever a man does, whatever motion he cherifhes in his heart of the vicious fpecies, whatever licence he gives to his paffions be-yond the bounds prefcribed by the divine law, operates as water on a flame; it damps its ardour. And we fee that thofe, who deviate from the paths of innocence, go on ftep by ftep, by little and little, till they are brought to actions of the moft cri-minal nature, deftructive of their health, deftructive of their fouls peace, and which af-ford them no pleafure, but a fearful look-ing for of the juft judgement of the divine Being who will deal with every man accor-ding to his works. I fay, every deviation

from

from the path of virtue will have this effect, to quench the fpirit. Let us, therefore, by every poffible means, endeavour
to cherifh this divine flame; it is a fpark
fent from heaven, and it is defigned to purify us throughout, to make us veffels holy
to the Lord, meet for an inheritance with
the faints in light, and to celebrate the
praifes of heaven's King for evermore.

Quench not the Spirit. Yield to that
monitor, which cautions you againft even
the appearance of evil, which is mercifully
given unto man to direct him in his courfe
in this world, and eftablifh him, happily
eftablifh him, in the life that is to come, in
the poffeffion of that fpecies of felicity,
which eye hath not feen, nor ear heard,
nor has it entered into the heart, the un-
converted heart, to conceive; but God
hath revealed it to us, fays the apoftle, by
his Spirit; for, the Spirit fearches all things,
yea, the deep things of God.

Quench not the Spirit. Add, to your
faith, virtue; to virtue, knowledge; to
knowledge,

knowledge, temperance; to temperance, brotherly kindnefs; to brotherly kindnefs, charity. Thus cherifh the holy flame; yield to the falutary influence of the Spirit, that quickeneth to cherifh in your breafts every heavenly and every friendly affection. The duty of a Chriftian, both with refpect to his Creator and his fellow-creature, is fet forth to us in the anfwer which our Lord gave to one who afked him, which is the greateft commandment ? *Thou fhalt love the Lord thy God with all thy heart, with all thy foul, and with all thy ftrength.* This is the firft and great commandment; and, the tendency of that Spirit which we have received, if we yield to its influence, would animate our affections toward that Being on whom we depend, and by whofe bleffings we are fupported; raife our minds to contemplate the inftances of God's power, righteoufnefs, goodnefs, and truth, manifefted; and enable us to afcend, as upon the wings of an eagle, in a meditation on the divine attributes; and infpire us with

M 3   that

that fpecies of gratitude which it is not in
the power of language to define.

*Thou fhalt love the Lord thy God with all
thy heart, with all thy foul, and with all thy
ftrength.* This is the firft and great commandment ; and this we fhould be inftructed to do, if we yielded to the influences of,
and did not quench, the Spirit, which is
like a fire to enkindle within us a facred
flame of devotion, in which we may en-
compafs the altar of the Almighty, in the
multitude of his mercies, and approach acceptably the temple of his holinefs.

Defpife not prophefying. Now it is to be
underftood, that the manifeftation of the
Spirit does not fuperfede, or render ufelefs,
inftrumental means. God has ufed both
thefe means ; he has fpoken unto our fathers by the prophets ; he has fpoken to us,
in thefe latter days, by his Son ; he has
fent his apoftles to go forth, by his authority, in his name, to *preach the Gofpel to the
poor, to heal the broken-hearted, to proclaim
liberty to the captive, the opening of the prifon*

to

to them who were bound, to proclaim the ac-
ceptable year of the Lord and the day of ven-
geance of our God. He appointed fome prophets, and fome evangelifts, and fome paf-
tors and teachers, for the edifying of the
body in that love by which it is united unto
its holy head. Defpife not therefore prophefying.

At the fame time that we conceive this
manifeftation of the Spirit to be the primary law and rule of our actions, we muft by
no means defpife inftrumental means of
inftruction. All Scripture is given by the
infpiration of God, and is profitable for
doctrine, for reproof, for correction, for
inftruction in righteoufnefs, to make the
man of God perfect, thoroughly furnifhed
unto all good works, and is able to make us
wife unto falvation, through faith which is
of Chrift Jefus: we therefore accept the Scriptures as an ineftimable bleffing; for, in them
we have an account of the various difpenfations of divine wifdom, and in which we
have the concurrent teftimony of the apof-

tles

tles and prophets of Jesus Christ to this fundamental principle of which we are most firmly persuaded.

Despise not prophesying. Let us improve, by every means which divine wisdom lays in the way, that we may be furnished to every good word and work, and increase in the knowledge of God.

Despise not prophesying; prove all things; hold fast that which is good. I conceive that the manifestation of the Spirit, given to every man to profit withal, is proposed to his rational understanding, and supersedes not the use of those rational powers by which he is distinguished ; but it qualifies him to exercise those powers in the best line and to the noblest purposes, to assert the dignity of his nature, and qualify him for those species of employments which are suited to the nature of an immortal spirit, made a little lower than the angels. He is to prove all things, and hold fast that which is good. The Father of lights appeals to the understanding and faculties of men ;

when

when he makes a revelation to his creatures, he mercifully condefcends to let himfelf down to the faculties they poffefs; he
fpeaks to them in a language they underftand. Therefore *prove all things*; diftinguifh properly between things and things
in matters of the greateft importance,
thofe which refpect our final acceptance
with the Judge of the whole earth. There
are none that claim more our ferious attention. They refpect not only the welfare of
our bodies in this world, but alfo the welfare of our fouls in that eternity, to the confines of which we are nearly approaching.
*Let every man, therefore, be fully perfuaded
in his own mind*; for, to him that knoweth
to do good, and doeth it not, to him it is
fin. Let us not be content with being the
nominal difciples of Chrift, but let us
confider ourfelves as capable of judging in
thofe matters that moft nearly concern us;
and, if any lack wifdom, let him afk it of
him who giveth liberally and upbraideth
not, and it fhall be given him. If we would
be

be inftructed in matters of everlafting importance, let us confult the facred oracle,
Chrift, within us, the hope of glory, and
who is faid to be within every man unlefs he
be a reprobate; for, fays the apoftle, *examine yourfelves, whether ye be in the faith;
prove your own felves; know ye not yourfelves,
how that Jefus Chrift is in you, except ye be
reprobates?*

It feems that our Saviour forefaw the di-
vifions that would foon commence among
mankind, and endeavoured to guard his
difciples againft the dogmas of men, and
turn them to fomething within them as a
fufficient guide and rule of their actions;
for, fays he, fome will fay, *lo! here is
Chrift; and others, lo! there is Chrift;* he is
to be found among the circle of profeffors;
lo! here is Chrift; others fay, lo! there is
Chrift; but go not forth after them, for,
the kingdom of God is within you. And
again, we are told, that that, which is to
be known of God, is manifeft: — where?
fhall we confult the many commentators
on

on the Old and New Teſtament? ſhall we traverſe the earth to ſearch into the opinions and modes of remote antiquity, in order to know what we ſhall do to be ſaved, or in order to know how we ſhal! be accepted of God? no: that, which is to be known of God, is manifeſted in man,—within. — Having made theſe obſervations, I recommend them to your conſideration.

Quench not the Spirit ; deſpiſe not propheſy- ing; prove all things, and hold faſt that which is good. And may we, individually, according to that light and manifeſtation of the Spirit which is given unto us, be faithful to the revelations communicated to us thereby, ſo that we may have the teſti- mony of a good conſcience ; and, when we have deviated, let us endeavour to poſſeſs thoſe penitential diſpoſitions, that, through Jeſus Chriſt, we may be accepted of God, and made meet for the realms of glory, where, with the general aſſembly and church of the firſt-born, and the ſpirits of juſt men made perfect, we may contem-

plate

plate the perfections of the divine Being, and may join the celeſtial hoſt in the ſong of Moſes, the ſervant of God, and the ſong of the Lamb, ſaying, *Great and mar-vellous are thy works, Lord God Almighty; juſt and true are thy ways, thou King of ſaints!*

PRAYER

P R A Y E R

A T T H E

CONCLUSION of the MEETING.

MOST gracious Father of all our mercies, unto whom we have accefs
through Jefus Chrift, thy Son, imprefs us
with a humbling fenfe of our own unworthinefs, and of thine infinite mercy and
goodnefs, that we may approach thine holy
altar, and humbly implore thee, the Fountain of wifdom and ftrength, that thou
wouldft be pleafed to enlighten our underftandings, that we may fee ourfelves as we
are

are feen of thee, and may abhor ourfelves as in duft and afhes, feeling all thofe penitential affections which may render us the objects of thy forgivenefs, through Jefus Chrift our Lord. Be pleafed to affift us with the aid of thy Holy Spirit, that, in the future part of our earthly pilgrimage, we may be able effectually to correct the errors which we have committed in the firft. — That, under the influence of thy grace, we may pafs the time of our fojourning here in fear, and may be ftrengthened to lay afide every weight, and the fin which doth moft eafily befet us, and run with patience the race which is fet before us, in hope of attaining the eternal inheritance that fadeth not away. Thou moft glorious Being, who art the fource of ftrength to the righteous in all generations, and the tower of their defence ; whofe bread fhall never fail them, and their waters fhall be fure ; look down upon us, and fend us help out of thy fanctuary, and ftrengthen us out of thy Sion, that we may be ftrong in the

the Lord, and in the power of his might, and be able to ftand againft the force of all thofe enemies who would impede our progrefs to the city of Jerufalem, the city of the faints folemnities. Be pleafed, O Lord, to conduct us by thy counfel, ftrengthen us by thy grace, and afterwards take us into the realms of celeftial glory; that, when thou fhalt call us hence, we may enter into thofe regions where there is fulnefs of joy; and where, with the general affembly and church of the firft-born, whofe names are written in heaven, and the fpirits of juft men made perfect, we may celebrate thy praife. It is with this view our fouls are proftrate before thee; and we would afcribe to thee, glory, majefty, and dominion, and every other excellent attribute of which thou art worthy, both now and for evermore. Amen.

DISCOURSE

DISCOURSE VIII.

WHEN I firſt entered under this roof, I felt as little difpofition to vocal public ſervice as any in the whole of this congregation could have poſſeſſed. Conſcious of my own weakneſs and my many infirmities, I ſecretly wiſhed to be ſtrengthened by him, who is the Miniſter of the ſanctuary and the glorious High Prieſt of the Chriſtian religion; and indeed, unleſs we are favoured with his preſence, we ſhall ſit as it were in darkneſs and in the regions of the ſhadow of death. If we feel not the

influence

influence of his Holy Spirit, effectually to quicken us and infpire us with the fpirit of devotion, in vain fhall we lift up our hands and offer up the facrifice of vocal prayer and praife unto him. It would be well if we had ever in remembrance, that of ourfelves we are nothing, and of ourfelves can do nothing, I mean nothing that is effentially good. Unlefs in our religious affemblies we are firft miniftered unto by the chief Shepherd and Bifhop of fouls, we cannot poffibly minifter one to another. This the apoftles very evidently fhew, particularly where one of them, alluding to his Gofpel-miniftry, fays, *that we may comfort others with the comfort wherewith we ourfelves are comforted of God.* The difciple muft firft receive of his Lord, before he can difpenfe it to his brethren. And it is therefore that we profefs, I fay profefs at leaft, to meet upon one common bottom, both minifters and thofe in a private ftation, to wait, in all finglenefs of heart, upon that Being, who regardeth the crying of the poor and

the

the fupplications of the needy ; who in a peculiar manner will look unto that man who is poor and of a contrite fpirit, and that trembleth at his word. And, *though the youth may faint, and the young men utterly fall, yet thofe, who wait upon the Lord, fhall renew their ftrength ; they fhall mount upwards with wings as eagles ; they fhall run, and not be weary ; they fhall walk, and not faint.*

It might perhaps be a little profitable for us to enquire what we are to underftand by the renewing of our ftrength : *they, that wait upon the Lord, fhall renew their ftrength.* I conceive this to be intended purely in a fpiritual fenfe ; for, if natural ftrength be exhaufted by labour or fatigue, it is to be recovered, in the ordinary courfe of God's providence, only by reft and the application of fuitable nutritious food ; but thofe, who wait upon the Lord, fhall renew their ftrength. Such are the nature and conftitution of the human foul, that, in order to be preferved and live to God,

N 2

with

with a holy zeal for his name and for his caufe, to be endowed with ftrength virtuoufly to refolve, and virtuoufly to purfue the juft man's way, it muft be renewed by food that is of a fpiritual nature; that, as bread is a term for natural food, which is adapted to the fupport and well-being of our bodies, fo this fpiritual food, renewed unto us by the renewings of the Holy Ghoft, is that bread which indeed the world knoweth not of. The world that lieth in wickednefs, the fenfualift, has no tafte nor relifh for that bread which cometh down from God out of heaven, and nourifheth the foul up unto eternal life.

Though, in the application which the difciples were inftructed to make to the common Father of us all, outward bleffings might be included with fpiritual ones, yet doubtlefs, as the welfare of the foul is of infinitely more importance than the health and welfare of the body, in that part of the prayer, in which we are inftructed to fay — Give us this day our daily bread, is

principally

principally intended that spiritual communication with the God of the spirits of all flesh, which imparts strength and vigour to the soul, animating it with a spirit of real devotion, that it can ascend above this lower and terrestrial sphere, — ascend as upon *the wings of an eagle*, a bird which is said to approach the nearest to that glorious natural luminary, the sun, in its flights. So, that soul, which possesses not only the spirit of real religion, but also feels its best affections animated towards God, will have this privilege over the mere professor of religion, that he will ascend as upon the wings of an eagle, ascend in an awful contemplation of the divine attributes, in a meditation upon spiritual subjects, in a strain of holy and fervent devotion; he will ascend the mount of the Lord's holiness, encompass his altar in the multitude of his mercies, and lift up his heart with his hands to that Being who inhabits the heavens.

Impressed with the importance of these truths, which we, as a religious society,

peculiarly

peculiarly profefs, let us, friends, not
come to their meetings merely with an expectation of receiving benefit, edification,
or comfort, one from another. Let us
not look one upon another with — *Men and*
brethren, what fhall we do to be faved? or,
who fhall fhew us any good ? But, fenfible
of our own refpective wants, and impreffed
with a juft idea of the folemnity of that
bufinefs which we are profeffedly met about,
let us, in the nothingnefs of felf, in the
filence of all flefh, reverently wait upon the
Minifter of the fanctuary ; and to him let
us look with all finglenefs of heart, and
fay, Lord, lift thou up the light of thy
countenance upon us. Thus, poffeffing
that affection of mind which is analogous
to the affection of corporal hunger, as perfons fenfible of our wants, and alfo where
thofe wants can be effectualiy fupplied, we
fhall become the objects of that moft defirable bleffing, *bleffed are thofe who hunger*
and thirft after righteoufnefs, for they fhall be
filled. It feems to me, beyond the leaft degree

gree of doubt, that the royal pfalmiſt felt this ſpiritual hunger; he felt this ſenſe of want, and the need that he ſtood in of a ſupply from the divine preſence, when he ſpeaks to this purport: *As the hart panteth after the water-brooks, ſo panteth my ſoul after thee, O God;* and again, *My ſoul thirſteth for God, yea, for the living God.* This paſſage of the royal pfalmiſt ſeems to convey an idea to me of the ſoul which feels the weight of its own infirmities, the preſſure and the importunity of ſurrounding temptations; cloſely preſſed, hunted as it were, purſued by its enemies, as the hart, when its ſtrength is nearly exhauſted, and almoſt ready to faint and drop with thirſt, to whom nothing could be more precious than a ſpring of water: therefore, as the hunted hart panteth after the water-brooks, ſo that ſoul, which is ſenſible of its infirmities, and feels the preſſure of ſurrounding temptations, longs after that immortal ſpring of goodneſs, where it may be refreſhed and ſtrengthened, and eſcape from its ene-

mies,

mies, to purfue its courfe fuccefsfully, and ultimately to finifh it with joy.

I wifh we were more and more imprefted with a juft fenfe of what we are, that the pride of human nature were more effectually humbled; — that we might look up to him who is the fource of all that is excellent and good, and, to ufe the language of the holy penman, *feel after the Lord, if haply we might find him.* And he, whom the fervent foul is in fearch after, is not afar off; he, whom thou longeft for, will fuddenly come unto his temple; but, *who fhall abide the day of his coming? who fhall ftand when he appeareth?* When the foul is thus favoured with a fpiritual communion and intellectual fenfe of the fupreme Being, it is then that every thing that is exalted becomes abafed; the loftinefs of man is brought down; he fees himfelf as a worm, and no man; as unworthy the leaft of his mercies and truth; and therefore, in this view of himfelf and of the fupreme Being, he will break forth, in the language of Job,

Job, *I have heard of thee by the hearing of the ear* ;—fo far the fpeculatift may go, fo far the theorift may collect a fyftem of faith ; but, he not only heard of him by the hearing of the ear, but, fays he, *now mine eye feeth thee.* He had formed juft notions of the fupreme Being ; he was enlightened to have juft ideas of himfelf. *I have heard of thee*, fays he, *by the hearing of the ear ; but now mine eye feeth thee ; wherefore I repent and abhor myfelf in duft and afhes.* This is that humbling fenfe which we all of us fhould poffefs of ourfelves, if, in the fenfe which our Saviour intended, we were favoured to fee God : *Bleffed* (fays he) *are the pure in heart, for they fhall fee God;* which certainly muft be intended in a peculiar and fpiritual fenfe, for he is not the object of our fenfes. To be fure, in one refpect, it may be faid, the pure and the impure fee God ; they have a fenfible demonftration of his being in the works of creation, and of the attributes of power, wifdom, and goodnefs; but they have not that animating, that intellectual,

tellectual, vifion, which is the blefling of the pure in heart: *Bleffed are the pure in heart, for they fhall fee God.* Let none be fo weak as to imagine this is to be underftood in the fulleft fenfe of the word; for, in the fupreme Being *we live, and move, and have our being*; he comprehends all things, and is comprehended by nothing. *If thou afcend up to heaven, he is there; if thou go down to the depth of the fea, he is there.* The darknefs and the light are both alike to him; he is infinite in all his attributes; he is omniprefent; he pervadeth every part of his vaft extended empire; there are no bounds to Omnipotence; he remains the fame from generation to generation; with him, the perfect King, there is no variablenefs, neither any fhadow of turning. When we contemplate with propriety the attributes of this Being through the fanctification of the Spirit, then we experience what it is to have a pure heart, a heart poffefling purity of intention, whofe faculties and powers are placed on a pure object,

and

and all under the influence of the Holy
Spirit, and under the government of thofe
laws which the infinitely-wife Legiflator
hath adapted to promote the happinefs of all
his creatures, and to prepare them for
the glory, and the dignity, that is the peculiar privilege of the pure in heart; the enjoyment of that pure ftate of being, which
we fee now but darkly, through a glafs,
where the wicked ceafe from troubling,
and the weary are at reft ; where the fociety
of the juft are employed in contemplating
the attributes of the eternal King, and join
in the *folemn fong of Mofes, the fervant of God,
and of the Lamb, faying, Great and marvellous are thy works, O Lord God Almighty;
juft and true are thy ways, thou King of
faints !*

PRAYER

PRAYER

CONCLUSION of the MEETING.

MOST gracious God, as of ourſelves we can do nothing, be pleaſed, we humbly beſeech thee, to look down from the heavens, the habitation of thy holineſs, favourably upon us at this ſeaſon. Do thou lift up the light of thy glorious coun-tenance upon us, that in thy light, O Lord, we may ſee light, and that our underſtand-ings may be effectually informed reſpecting thoſe things which belong to our peace and

to

to thy glory; that our underſtandings may not only be enlightened to ſee, but alſo our hearts ſtrengthened and animated to engage in the work of righteouſneſs, which is peace, and the effect of it quietneſs and aſſurance for ever.

O moſt merciful Father, look down upon us, vile unworthy creatures; inflame our hearts with a ſenſe of gratitude to thee, the Author and Fountain of every good and perfect gift, of all thoſe bleſſings which we have received, and have ſo much miſapplied, in the courſe of our ſhort pilgrimage; that, under a juſt ſenſe of thy majeſty, of thy mercy and goodneſs, and of our own weakneſs, we may be induced to approach thy holy altar, and put up our ſupplications unto thee, that thou wouldeſt be pleaſed to ſend us health out of thy ſanctuary, and ſtrengthen us as out of Zion.

Thou, that haſt been a rock and a place of refuge for the righteous in all generations, look down, we beſeech thee, upon thoſe that are under the preſſure of any ſpecies

cies of affliction and probation, thofe whofe hearts are right towards thee, who are going to Mount Sion, and have had their feet directed thither. Oh ! be pleafed to afford thefe the aid of thy Spirit in the moments of human weaknefs, and in their folemn adverfe feafon. Lift up the light of thy countenance upon them. O Lord, preferve us all in the courfe of our pilgrimage through this vale of tears ; guide us, by the light of thy counfel, and afterwards receive us into the realms of celeftial glory, where, having been previoufly effectually purged, fanctified, and juftified, in and through thy Son, our Lord and Saviour, Jefus Chrift, we may join the heavenly fociety, and for ever be with the faints and angels, and fpirits of juft men made perfect, to laud and praife thy great and excellent name ; to whom, for all thy mercies, be the dominion, thankfgiving, blefling, and praife, not only now, but henceforth and for evermore. Amen.

DISCOURSE

DISCOURSE IX.

THIS do, and thou shalt live. These words of our Lord revived in my remembrance at this meeting, and I have been led to advert to the occasion of their being delivered. It is, I think, written in one of the evangelists: *Behold, a certain lawyer stood up, and tempted him, saying, Master, what shall I do to inherit everlasting life?* It is written, that he meant to tempt him; it follows of course, that his motive, in proposing this question, was not of the best kind; that it was not with a view of gaining information, but, if possible, to ensnare him, and

take

take an occafion againft him. But, our
Lord, upon this as well as upon every other
occafion, manifefted that wifdom which he
poffeffed above all other men, that wifdom
which directed all that he did and all that
he faid; *he fpoke as never man fpoke;* he
fpoke with peculiar authority, and not as
the fcribes. Inftead of making an immediate and direct anfwer to this queftion, he
previoufly propofed one to him. *What,*
fays he, *is written in the law? how readeft
thou?* To which the lawyer replied, *Thou
fhalt love the Lord thy God with all thy heart,
and with all thy foul, and with all thy ftrength,
and with all thy mind, and thy neighbour as
thyfelf.* To which Jefus faid, *Thou haft anfwered right; this do, and thou fhalt live.* It
feemeth to me, that this lawyer might apprehend, as fome others did who had a
prejudice againft Jefus, and the worthy
caufe which he promoted upon the earth,
that he came to deftroy the law and the
prophets, and to preach another law effentially different from that which had been

delivered

delivered to them; or that he difpenfed with the obligation of that, which, by way of diftinction, is called the moral law. But our Saviour evinced that he came not to deftroy the law, but to fulfil it; he told them, that heaven and earth fhould fooner pafs away than one jot or tittle of the law fhould fail. Now the law which our Saviour intended, when he fays, *What is written in the law? how readeft thou?* could not be any part of the new Teftament, becaufe none of that had been written; he therefore intended that law of commandments which is of univerfal and indifpenfable obligation, and is immutable: *Thou fhalt love the Lord thy God with all thy heart, and with all thy foul, and with all thy ftrength, and with all thy mind; and thy neighbour as thyfelf.* Now we are inftructed that love is the fulfilling of the law; but in what fenfe is it the fulfilling of the law? why, whoever poffeffes the love of God will be induced, by the beft motives, to ftudy his will, and to difcharge the obligation of his feve-

O ral

ral religious duties to him.—If he loves his neighbour, he will be induced to defire his welfare on all occafions. He will feek the intereft and good of his neighbour; he will not only be juft, but merciful, kind, and loving. And this definition perfectly agrees with that paffage where it is faid, *Love worketh no ill to his neighbour*.

Now I conceive that there is no other way for us to obtain that moft defirable object of being accepted of our Creator, who is the Judge of the whole earth, than to obferve thofe facred commandments on which hang all the law and the prophets. And it feems to me, that there is much more of the love of God and the love of our neighbour affumed, or profeffed, than is really poffeffed at heart by mankind. The pride, the haughtinefs, the irreverence, with which they appear in the prefence of the omnifcient Being, befpeak that they poffefs not the love of him in their hearts. Ambition, avarice, and the various fpecies of vanity which have invaded the feveral claffes of

mankind,

mankind, befpeak that they are void of the
love of the God of heaven and of the
whole earth. They, who rife up early,
and go to bed late, in order to add houfe to
houfe, and barn to barn, and bag to bag,
and land to land, till there is nothing left
for the poor of the earth ; who improve
every opportunity to monopolize as much
as poffible the bleffings of heaven, and
whofe thirft feems to be inexhauftible ; who
are prompted by avarice, which is a paffion
that increafes with the increafe of years,
and increafes with the increafe of riches;
manifeft that the love of God is not in
them : for, the apoftle faith, *If any man love
the world, the love of the Father is not in him*;
by which I underftand, if a man is poffeffed
of an inordinate love of the things of this
world ; if they fo take hold of his affections, and ingrofs his attention, as to fteal
from him that awe of God which ever
ought to pervade his foul ; if it prevents
his attention to the ftatutes and the commandments of heaven, and prevents his

O 2 walking

walking humbly and reverently through this short scene of his pilgrimage; it is, and may be justly called, that kind of love of the world which excludes the love of the supreme Being.

But, while it is so little, I fear, possessed at heart, much is professed by all the several denominations of religion; however they may differ with respect to speculative tenets, certain rituals, and modes of devotion, and articles of faith, they all profess to love God, all acknowledge the obligation of that and of the subsequent commandment; but it is to be feared that we often treat the supreme Being in a manner similar to that which we use one towards another. Among mankind, there are great and specious pretences of friendship, when perhaps there is but little really possessed at heart; and indeed some, under the semblance of love and friendship, have only waited for an opportunity to stab the reputation, or injure their neighbour in his property or person, with security from the lash of the law.

law. There are, who have made this pro-
feſſion as a cloak of maliciouſneſs; and,
while they have ſaid, Art thou in health,
brother? have had a dagger concealed beneath the black diſguiſe. Now we are
abundantly inſtructed, that, though we
may, and too frequently do, deceive one
another, and paſs off baſe metal for ſter-
ling coin, yet it is impoſſible we ſhould deceive that awful Being with whom we have
to do; he ſees not as man ſees; he looks
beyond the veil of every covering; he be-
holds the latent receſſes of the human
heart. Let us therefore not be deceived,
for God is not mocked; that which every
man ſows, that ſhall he reap; if he ſows
unto the fleſh, he ſhall of the fleſh reap
corruption; but, if he ſows unto the Spirit, of the Spirit he ſhall reap life everlaſting.

In vain ſhall we call upon the name of
the Lord, in vain ſhall we ſacrifice upon his
altar, in vain ſhall we make many prayers,
and ſpread our hands towards the habita-

tion

tion of his holiness, unless we possess the love of him in the highest; and which, whoever possesses, he will manifest in the various branches of life, his conversation, and commerce among mankind. He will conscientiously discharge his religious, his social, his relative, duties ; and, in the sphere of his movement, he will manifest the love of God by keeping his commandments. *If ye love me,* (says our Lord,) *keep my commandments* ; and, if we would really become objects of his complacency, if we would be loved and honoured of that Being who made us for the purpose of his own glory, let us attend to the solemn injunction of the Author of the Christian religion : *Keep you therefore my commandments and abide in my love, even as I have kept my Father's commandments and abide in his love.*

Let us not therefore apprehend, that any articles of faith, that any rituals of devotion, or any form of prayer that can possibly be uttered, can be a substitute for this affection

affection of heart towards God, and which the confideration of his attributes will the moft powerfully engage us to poffefs. We have nothing that we have not received; he, the Ancient of days, is the fole proprietor of the univerfe, the Lord of hofts; he is one, and his name is one. We, the inhabitants of his footftool, are but tenants at will. The earth is the Lord's, and the fulnefs thereof, and the cattle of a thoufand hills are his. And, feeing we poffefs nothing but what we have derived from him, that all the bleffings which we have received are owing to his bounty and goodnefs, we ought not to boaft as if we had not received them, but with all humility acknowledge his manifold goodnefs, and to offer unto him the facrifice of an undivided heart. It is the language of Wifdom to the fons of men, *My fon, give me thy heart.* Our beft affections will be engaged; then, indeed, we fhall poffefs the very fpirit of devotion; for, whoever poffeffes not the love of God poffeffes not the fpirit of devo-

O 4   tion;

tion ; his hands may be lifted up towards the habitation of his holinefs, but his heart lies groveling on the earth ; he is worfhipping the gods of this world, filver and gold, and therefore the lifting up of his hands and the verbal oblation of his mouth will not be acceptable incenfe upon that facred altar, whereof thofe who ferve the tabernacle have no right to partake.

I wifh that we might improve fuch feafons as this in a particular manner, to contemplate the divine attributes, to reflect and think upon his name, to recollect the inftances of his goodnefs, of his power, and of his wifdom, that fo we may feel our affections more and more fet upon things that are above, lefs and lefs upon things which are beneath, which are but of a tranfitory nature, and which perifh with the ufing. This was the injunction of the apoftle : *Set your affection on things above, and not on things on the earth.* This indeed is to be fpiritually minded, as it is written,

to

to be carnally minded is death, but to be spiritually minded is life and peace.

If we were really concerned to poffefs this love of God, it would not only manifeft itfelf in the various branches of our religious duty, but alfo thofe of a focial and relative kind. I think we are fomewhere told, that, for a man to fee his fellow-creature in diftrefs, and fhut up his bowels againft him, how dwelleth the love of God in him? and the apoftle reafons very aptly: *If*, fays he, *we love not our brother, whom we have feen, how fhall we love God, whom we have not feen*, who is not an object of fenfe, who is inapproachable? no man hath feen him, nor can fee him; and, as we are incapable of rendering any thing unto God, who is abfolutely perfect, it feems that he accepts of the good offices we do for one another as if they had been done unto him, and he was capable of being benefited by them. This is illuftrated by our Lord with refpect to thofe who had neglected him: *I was an-hungered, and ye fed me not; naked,*

and

*and ye clothed me not; sick and in prison,
and ye visited me not;* to which they made
this reply: *When saw we thee an-hungered, or
naked, or sick, or in prison, and did not minister
unto thee? —* Inasmuch, says he, *as ye did it
not to one of the least of these my brethren, ye
did it not unto me;* and again, to those who
received him, it is said, *I was an-hungered,
and ye fed me; naked, and ye clothed me,* or
words to the same import; *I was sick and in
prison, and ye visited me.* Now these possessed that modesty which is peculiar to
good men; they answered: *When saw we
thee an-hungered, or naked, or sick, or in prison, and ministered unto thee?* Inasmuch,
says he, *as ye have done it to one of the least
of these little ones, you have done it to me. —*
Who are these little ones? I conceive that
we are all, by creation, God's little ones;
he stands in the relation of a father to all
ranks and classes of human beings; he of
one blood has made all nations to dwell on
all the face of the earth, and hath determined the times before appointed, and the
bounds

bounds of their habitation; and, as he has made them of one blood, so he looks upon them with an everlafting love, which difcriminates not the perfons of men; for, he is no refpecter of perfons; but, in every nation, he, that feareth God and worketh righteoufnefs, is accepted of him. And, that the little ones, in this place, intend not any peculiar clafs, to me is very evident; becaufe, we are under an obligation to do good to the unrighteous as well as the righteous, to the unjuft as well as the juft; not only to be loving to our friends, but to love our enemies, to do good to all; to put up our prayers, not for this or that peculiar clafs of perfons, but to addrefs our prayers for the vaft community of creatures: — *I exhort,* fays the apoftle, *that prayers and fupplications be made for all men; for kings, and for all that are in authority; that we may lead a quiet and peaceable life, in all godlinefs and honefty.* We are to pray for the righteous, that they may be confirmed in their ways; — for the wicked, that they

may

may be reformed. We are to pray not only for our friends, for, if we love them that love us, what do we more than others? It is natural to have an affection for them who have an affection for us ; but we muft go farther than this, we muft love them that hate us, and pray for them that perfe- cute us. If we poffefs this fpirit of mind, if love prevails to all, then we fhall ever have occafion, as our Lord faid, rather to rejoice than to be forrowful if we fhall be mal-treated by thofe whofe intereft we have endeavoured to promote : — *Bleffed are ye* (fays our Lord) *when men fhall fay all man- ner of evil againft you, falfely, for my fake ; rejoice and be exceeding glad, for great is your reward in heaven.* Now I wifh that this af- fection of love, the love of God and of our neighbour, were more really felt at heart than it appears to be.

The love of our neighbour means not, in the common acceptation of the term, the people whofe local habitation is near ours, and who lend us fome affiftance, as

we

we are inftructed in the cafe of the Samaritan and the poor Jew, when it was afked
our Lord, who is my neighbour? It feemed good fometimes to him to anfwer the
queftions propofed to him by a parable. It
was peculiar to thofe times and that part
of the world; and, fo frequent was it, that
it is faid of our Lord, that without a parable fpake he not unto them. A certain
man, fays he, went down from Jerufalem
to Jericho, and fell among thieves, who
ftripped him, and wounded him, and departed, leaving him half dead. Here was
an object for Chriftian benevolence to exercife itfelf upon; here was an inftance in
which the love of our neighbour fhould
have been exercifed; but it feems that
thofe, who ought to have poffeffed the
greateft fhare of friendly affections, thofe
who waited upon the fervice of the altar,
wanted this affection. The prieft paffed
by, the Levite followed his example; thofe,
who ought to have been the firft to fet an
example of mercy, loving-kindnefs, and
charity,

charity, poffeffed not that affection, which would engage us, by every means in our power, to relieve the diftreffed and wipe away the tears of the afflicted. In fhort, fo much ftrefs is laid upon the poffeffion of this affection, and exercifing it in charity and kindnefs one towards another, that it is faid to be the religion which is pure and undefiled, not a religion of fpeculation and theory: *Pure religion, and undefiled before God and the Father, is this: to vifit the fatherlefs and widows in their affliction, and to keep ourfelves unfpotted from the world.*

The prieft paffed by; the Levite alfo paffed by. At length, it feems, a Samaritan came that way; and, though there had long fubfifted an enmity between the Jews and the Samaritans, yet he poffeffed fo much of the love of God and his neighbour, that it overcame the prejudice of his education; though the object that claimed this attention was a Jew, he took compaffion on him in this ftate, and did not, as we often do to one another, pour in a mixture

ture of wormwood and gall, to aggravate the wounds, rather than the oil of love, to alleviate and affuage them. He poured in oil and wine; and not only fo, but he looked forwards, and provided for his future fubfiftence; he fent him to an inn, and, when he departed, directed the hoft to take care of him, faying, Whatfoever thou fpendeft, when I come again, I will repay thee.

This is fet forth as an example to us, which we fhould by all means attempt to imitate. We fhould be divefted of every fpecies of prejudice, and endeavour to have our hearts more enlarged in the love of God; and, the more we are enlarged in the love of God, the more fhall we poffefs the love of our neighbour, and more promote the intereft of the vaft community of mankind, and be more difpofed to imitate the example of the Saviour of mankind among the poor and defpifed, who was, on that account, in reproach, called the friend of publicans and finners. We fhould exercife our

gifts

gifts for the promotion of righteousness on the earth, to prevent every calamity, and promote the intereft of fociety. It fhould be the ftudy of our lives, and our delight, to go about doing good. I am thankful I poffefs that fpirit of charity that forgets all the diftinctions of names, of rank, and of dignity. As men are ftripped of thefe diftinctions, and remember that they ftand in the relation of children to the Father of mankind, fo will their love and benevolence be; if we poffeffed this affection, we fhould endeavour to promote concord among the feveral ranks of fociety.

I wifh we may fee the reftoration of thofe primæval days, when the morning-ftars fang together, and all the fons of God fhouted for joy. — God is love; that is a term which is moft aptly applied, and moft glorioufly illuftrates the attributes of the fupreme Being. We are the offspring of his benevolence; it was to communicate happinefs, it was from the fource of his infinite benevolence, that he created us, and endued

endued us with capacities of partaking of the happiness of immortality. He has called us to keep his ftatutes, that we may poffefs a fpecies of happinefs inconceivable to us at prefent, and which, in its duration, will run parallel with the endlefs ages of eternity.

Seeing we have received every thing we poffefs from him, let us be proftrate at his footftool; let us, in all the emotions of filial piety, approach his altar, in the multitude of his mercies, and lift up our hands to the habitation of his holinefs ;— not only our hands, but alfo our hearts. *Lift up your hands and hearts to God,* I think the Pfalmift fays, *who inhabits the heavens.* — Thefe will be feafons of folemnity. We fhall enter into the clofets of our hearts, and fhut the door; we fhall be lifted up, as on the wings of an eagle, in the contemplation of his attributes, agreeable to the declaration of the prophet, who fpoke in the name of the Lord: *Though the youth may faint, and the young men utterly fall, yet they*

P   *who*

*who wait upon the Lord ſhall renew their
ſtrength ; they ſhall mount up with wings as
eagles ; they ſhall run, and not be weary ; they
ſhall walk, and not faint.* In holy fervour
of ſpirit, we ſhall be able to enter into that
within the vail, and in the depth of humiliation we ſhall worſhip the Lord in the
beauty of holineſs. Thus ſhall we be qualified to join the celeſtial ſong : *Glory to
God in the higheſt ; on earth, peace ; and good
will towards men.*

Under the ſenſe of theſe things, the manifeſtation of his preſence, and a participation of that food which is of a ſpiritual nature, the bread that cometh down from
God out of heaven, we ſhall be qualified
to approach him, not in a formal manner,
but the language of our hearts will be :

 ` *Our Father, who art in heaven, hallowed
be thy name ; thy kingdom come ; thy will be
done on earth as it is in heaven. Give us, this
day, our daily bread ; and forgive us our
treſpaſſes as we forgive them that treſpaſs
againſt us ; and, lead us not into temptation, but.*
:
                                                    deliver

deliver us from evil; for, thine is the kingdom, and the power, and the glory, for ever and ever. Amen.

PRAYER

PRAYER

AT THE

CONCLUSION of the MEETING.

MOST gracious God, infpire us more and more with fuitable affections towards thee, that we may find accefs to thy prefence, and offer up the acceptable incenfe of thankfgiving and of praife. O thou omnifcient Being, who knoweft us altogether as we are, grant, we befeech thee, that, under the influence of the light of the Gofpel of thy Son, we may fee ourfelves as we are feen of thee; that,

in

in the depth of reverence, we may abhor ourfelves in duft and afhes; that the re-membrance of our paft tranfgreffions, which have loudly befpoken our ingratitude to thee, thou moft adorable Being, may be blotted out; and that we may feel that contrition of foul, which becomes every penitent who is the proper object of thy mercy. O let the confideration of thine attributes and of our own unworthinefs humble us yet more and more in thy pre-fence; that, poffeffed with a filial fear of thee, we may in future be more circum-fpect in our goings; and that we may feek, and be able to difcriminate, the juft man's way, and to walk in it, which, as the bright and fhining light, fhineth more and more unto the perfect day. O grant that we may be more and more enamoured with the love of virtue; that we may more and more prefer the narrow and the ftrait gate, which leads to life, rather than the broad way of fenfual indulgence, that leads to the gates of death, and ultimately will in-

P 3   volve

volve fuch as perfevere therein in the pit of
perdition.

O moft adorable Jefus, increafe our
faith and love, and increafe the friendly affections of our fouls one towards another,
that we may be difpofed, inftead of bur-
dening others, to bear each others bur-
dens; inftead of cafting about to enfnare
and deceive, we may look upon our neighbours intereft as our own; that we may
promote the intereft of righteoufnefs in the
world; that, under the influence of the
Holy Spirit, through grace, we may walk
before thee fo, in this world, as to have an
ample hope of being received into the affembly of the juft in the life to come.

O thou, who art the preferver of men,
influence us more and more by thy Spirit,
that we may lay afide every weight and every burden, and the fin which doth fo eafily
befet us; and run with patience the race
which is fet before us; and fo to run, as
that we may obtain the crown immortal,
that fhall never fade away. While we are
fojourners

fojourners in this world, and in the land of the fhadow of death, open to us the brighter profpect of a fairer day ; that, whatfoever may be our lot in this pilgrimage, whether perfecution or diftrefs, we may have an intereft in thy Son, as a hope firm and fteadfaft, as an anchor in this tempeftuous ocean. Grant that, when the days of our pilgrimage are concluded, we may receive the end of our faith, even the falvation of our fouls, where the righteous fhall fhine as the brightnefs of the firmament, and as the ftars, for ever and ever.

O thou moft righteous Being, in a fenfe of thy goodnefs we would approach thy altar, and afcribe to thee might, majefty, and dominion, with every other excellent and adorable attribute, now, henceforth, and for evermore. Amen.

DISCOURSE X.

UNDER an apprehenfion of duty, I
have frequently laboure.i among you,
in word and doctrine, for a feries of years.
What effect it has had on thofe who have
heard me, I cannot prefume to determine;
if I were, indeed, to judge by appearances,
I fhould conclude the obvious effects to be
but little. But, there is a matter on which
I am fully competent to determine: my motives have been of the beft kind, the love of
God and the love of my fellow-creatures;
that love which worketh no ill, but would,
by all poffible methods, promote the effential

tial intereſt of its neighbours ; and, having from time to time diſcharged what I apprehended to be my religious duty, I have. therein found great peace. This, to myſelf at leaſt, has been the effeЄt of my public labours ; and, though it is probable, that what I have ſometimes delivered may have been more or leſs ſimilar to that which I have aforetime delivered, yet I hope, that even a repetition of doЄtrines and advices, which we are urged to deliver from a ſenſe of duty, may not be as water ſpilt upon a ſtone, but may have a tendency (if not to convey any material information to the underſtanding) to ſtir up at leaſt the pure mind by way of remembrance.

We have heard much ; we have had line upon line, and precept upon precept ; and there have been ſent among us, who, as good ſcribes, out of their treaſury have brought forth things new and old. But, the eſſential and important doЄtrines, which reſpeЄt in particular our praЄtical duties, make, it is to be feared, but a ſlight im
preſſion

preffion on the minds of men, even upon
thofe who are very fond of hearing, and
have perhaps much to fay concerning the
myfteries of faith; who, whilft they lay
much ftrefs upon fpeculative opinions, have
poffeffed too little of that real Chriftian
love and zeal, which manifefts itfelf by a
conduct confiftent with the commandments
of the Author of the Chriftian difpenfation. We want to be ftirred up, to be
excited, to do that, which we want not to
be inftructed it is our duty to do. But, if
there be any, in this auditory, whofe underftandings may have been bewildered in a
long and tedious purfuit of fpeculative notions; or who have attempted, though but
with little fuccefs, to inveftigate abftrufe
points, and to comprehend myfteries which
the wifdom of the Holy Ghoft may fee meet
to conceal from the foolifhnefs of men,
(the prying curiofity of the creature, who is
more apt to inquire than to obey;) if there
be any fuch, who are yet unfatisfied with
regard to thofe grand and effential points,
upon

upon which their acceptance with the common Father of the human race depends : if there be any who are under the preſſure of manifold ſins and tranſgreſſions, are in doubt with reſpeſt to thoſe means which are neceſſary to be purſued, in order that their tranſgreſſions may be forgiven of God, and that they may be accepted of him ; if there be any, who, in the anguiſh of their ſouls, have their hands upon their loins, with *what ſhall I do to be ſaved?* it ſeems to me to be my duty to ſtate to them a caſe, nearly perhaps as we have it repreſented in the holy Scriptures, reſpeſting one, formerly, who propoſed a queſtion of this ſort.

How ſhall I come before the Lord? or wherewithal ſhall I bow myſelf before the moſt high God? Shall I come before him with burnt offerings and calves of a year old? ſhall I preſent him with ten thouſands of rivers of oil? ſhall I give him my firſt-born for my tranſgreſſion, the fruit of my body for the ſin of my ſoul? — Now it ſeems to me, beyond

all

all controverfy, that, by *coming before the Lord, bowing before the moft high God*, was meant, the bowing before him, or coming before him, acceptably. What fhall I do to recommend myfelf to the divine notice, to have the load of my fins taken off? my tranfgreffions cancelled from the book of his remembrance? In anfwer to this, he was fhewn that that which God required of man, as effential to his acceptance with him, was eafily to be apprehended, and within the compafs of his power to perform; that is to fay, of man, favoured with the manifeftation of the Spirit of God, and ftrengthened by his grace.

He hath fhewed thee, O man! what is good; and what doth the Lord require of thee, but to do juftly, and to love mercy, and to walk humbly with thy God? Here our effential duties are fummed up under three heads, which indeed comprehend much. — The firft is *juftice*. A man muft be morally juft before he can be religioufly good; whereas we oft-times fee the divine order perverted, and ·that

that men are more zealous to be connected
with parties, and more zealous for the intereft of a fect, than to maintain even the
character of common honefty.

Do juftly.—Now the obligation of juftice
is void of any kind of perplexity. We no
fooner reflect upon the relation man ftands
in to man, but the propriety of juftice is
clear. We are without excufe if we neglect
to do juftice; and, though this perhaps
may come under the appellation of what is
called a moral duty, let us not think mean-
ly of moral duties; for, notwithftanding
the variety of fpeculative doctrines publifhed here and there, and curious diftinctions
made upon points of religion, what is the
ftate of moral juftice among us? Let us
look abroad among mankind; fhall we not
have caufe to apprehend, of many, that
their wits are employed, and time laid out,
in planning fchemes to take advantage of
their neighbours? in laying a foundation
to raife themfelves on the fpoils of others?
to make themfelves rich, and thereby fall

into

into many foolifh and hurtful lufts, which drown men in fin and perdition? ——— It feems to be the ftudy of a great part of mankind to outwit and deceive the other; inftances of notorious breaches of juftice ftrike us on every hand, and every where, and which people are the more prompted to commit from a defire of a luxurious and pompous mode of life, which is too generally prevalent among mankind. The difeafe of luxury is almoft epidemical; — through all claffes there feems to be an emulation to excel, and many burft in the attempt.

I am concerned at heart, friends, to revive in your remembrance the obligation of juftice. We muft be juft and righteous before we fhall be good; and it feems that our Lord laid a peculiar ftrefs on what are called moral doctrines, that of juftice and that of mercy; infomuch that he fays, *If ye forgive not men their trefpaffes, neither will your Father forgive your trefpaffes;* and again he fays, (which is worthy of note; it is called

the

the golden rule ; it is a law, a general law, of action, worthy of the Moſt High to give, and of his Son to promulgate among the inhabitants of the earth,) *Whatſoever ye wou'd that men ſhould do to you, do ye even ſo to them.* Here is the eſſence of all the beſt human laws or ſtatutes that ever were compoſed in the world. All human laws, ſo far as they are conſiſtent with propriety, are founded in, and conſiſtent with, this general law, which comprehends all relations and connections among mankind : — *Whatſoever ye would that men ſhould do to you, do ye even ſo to them.* If we would wiſh to appear with honeſty to our neighbours, let us act in the manner we would wiſh them to act to us. If we would wiſh them not to take advantage of us, let us not take advantage of them. As, in a time of diſtreſs, we would wiſh to have the ſympathy of our neighbours and the hand of relief extended to us, let us not forget the needy in the time of our proſperity, but do to them as we would they ſhould do to us. If we wiſh,

wifh, being in danger, to be apprifed of
that danger, that we might not fall into deftruction, let us warn and admonifh o-
thers. There is a mutual dependence runs
through fociety, and it is our duty to ad-
vertife one another in hours of peril ; and,
where we can do no pofitive good, we
fhould endeavour to prevent all poffible e-
vil. Thefe are duties which we want not
fo much to be convinced of, as to be effectually incited to perform. But, fuch is
the weaknefs of human nature, that people are more fond of taking up with fub-
fcriptions to articles of faith, and of attendance to ordinances, and wifh to get rid of
their fins in that way, and herein fhew a
great zeal ; but that falls fhort of the rectitude which the gofpel enjoins, and is the
end of the law, and the end of the coming
of Chrift, and of offering himfelf a facrifice for fin to produce order and righteoufnefs among all ranks of men. This was
one of the ends of his coming ; and, however fpecious our profeffions may be, how-

Q   ever

ever deeply we may enter into the myfteries of the kingdom of heaven, yet, if we pof-fefs not the fpirit of charity, and motives to juftice and benevolence, what is it? *If I fpeak,* fays the apoftle, *with the tongues of men and of angels, and have not charity, I am become as founding brafs or a tinkling cymbal; and, though I have the gift of prophecy, and underftand all myfteries, and all knowledge, and though I have all faith, fo that I could remove mountains, and have not charity, I am nothing.* By charity, I conceive, is not meant a guft of paffion that would prompt a man occafionally to do a good act, but a fettled principle of goodnefs and benevolence, that would prompt a man to general juftice, and not to be juft only, but alfo good. *If I fpeak with the tongues of men and of angels, and have not charity, it will profit me nothing; if I have all faith, and underftand all myfteries, yet,* fays he, *if I have not charity, it profiteth me nothing;* to fhew, that, in order to our actions being denominated good, they muft proceed from a good

motive

motive and principle. He ſhews that the
ſemblance of charity is nothing : *If I give
my body to be burned, and my goods to the poor,
and have not charity, it profiteth me nothing.*
Therefore, let us endeavour to be really
that we ſeem to be. Let us not content
ourſelves with the ſemblance of holineſs,
and charity, but let us hold the myſtery of
the faith in a pure conſcience : for, it is
poſſible people may conceive right notions
of things, and yet, for want of receiving
them as a principle influencing their actions, they may hold the truth, but hold it
in unrighteouſneſs ; but he, who holds the
myſtery of faith as he ought to hold it,
holds it in a pure conſcience.

Our Saviour, in his miniſtry, was gentle
in his addreſs, and perſuaſive in his language. When he addreſſed the publicans
and ſinners, he found more openneſs to receive the goſpel among this rank of people, than thoſe who had the form of godli-
neſs, but denied the power thereof ; inſo-
much, that it became a proverb, that he

was

was the friend of publicans and finners; for which conduct he gave this effential reafon, that he came not to call the righteous, but finners, to repentance. *Where the carcafe is, there will the eagles be gathered together.* Among thefe people there was a difpofition to receive him ; and, among other things which the meffengers of John were required to teftify that they had feen, was, that the poor had the gofpel preached to them. How did this friend of publicans and finners, who fpoke with fo much gentlenefs, behave when he came to addrefs the fuperior characters, in all the pomp of their fanctity, who made broad the phylacteries, who were zealous for the written and oral traditions of their fathers ? *O ye generation of vipers, how can ye efcape the damnation of hell ! Ye are like whited fepulchres, which, indeed, appear beautiful outward, but are within full of dead mens bones.* And he takes occafion to inftruct his followers, *unlefs,* fays he, *your righteoufnefs exceed the righteoufnefs of the Scribes and Pharifees,*

fees, you shall not enter into the kingdom of heaven. Now, what was the righteousnefs of the Scribes and Pharifees ? It feems they appeared more than a little zealous for- the rituals of the Mofaic difpenfation, were punctual to the time of prayer, fpecious in their addrefs to the Majefty of heaven, and performed all the fervice of the Jewifh tabernacle ; but, though they pofleffed the righteoufnefs of the law, they were ftrangers to moral righteoufnefs. *Ye pay tithe of mint, and annife, and cummin,* fays he, *but what have you neglected to do ? Ye have omitted the weightier matters of the law, judgement, mercy, and truth : thefe ought ye to have done, and not to leave the other undone :* by which, he does not reprehend them for their performance of the rituals of that difpenfation, which were obligatory until the facrifice of Chrift, yet he fhews the fuperiority of moral and practical truths, mercy and judgement. *Thefe ought ye to have done;* and, therefore, in point of order, when the prophet anfwers

the

the queſtion propoſed to him, the firſt is, *do juſtice:* which I conceive not only comprehends the obligation we owe to one another, but the obligation we owe to the Supreme Being. While I am zealous to plead for the obligation of juſtice among men, and the diſcharge of the duties of ſocial relations, I would by no means forget that there is a juſtice due to the glorious father of all we poſſeſs. He has made us, not we ourſelves ; we are his offspring ; he has communicated to us a variety of temporal and ſpiritual bleſſings, and we ought, in point of gratitude, in point of juſtice, to make a proper application of thoſe bleſſings, to render to him the duty that ariſes from the relation that we ſtand in to him as his children, the offspring of the everlaſting Father ; and, therefore, he calls upon us, *my ſon, give me thy heart.* He would not require that of us which is not in point of juſtice our duty to comply with : give me thy heart ; give me the beſt of thy affections ; manifeſt thy love to me by keep-

ing

ing my commandments, as a good steward;
for, we are all, all ranks and classes of beings are, stewards of the manifold grace of
God; and it is required of stewards that
they be found faithful. The time is ap-
proaching, when it will be said, *give an account of thy stewardship; for, thou mayst be no
longer steward.* Let us, therefore, ask ourselves this question,— what have we received? what improved? and what misap-
plied? and then ask, what owest thou to
my Lord? The debt is immense. We
have received much: our improvements
have been little; but wherewith shall we
come before the Most High? In what way
will the Father of mercies be propitious to
us? Let us first confess our faults; let us
not cover our sins, or seek to hide them;
for, he that hides his sins shall not prosper:
let us acknowledge our sins; let us
encompass his altar in the multitude
of his mercies; let us possess the penitential affection of the poor publican, while
the Pharisee could boast of his fasting twice
in the week, giving alms of all he possessed,

and

and not being as other men, even as the poor publican. Notwithftanding thefe pompous words, he was not accepted. The poor publican had nothing to plead, no merit to recommend him ; and, therefore, under the contemplation of the infinite Majefty he was about to approach, he had not courage to lift up his hands towards the habitation of his holinefs; but, fighing, faid, *Lord, be merciful to me, a finner !* If we poffefs thefe penitential affections, we fhall become the objects of that mercy which our Lord and Saviour Jefus Chrift exemplified in his miniftry, in his character, in his crucifixion, in his refurrection, and afcenfion into glory. It is a faithful faying, and worthy of all acceptation, that Jefus Chrift came into the world to fave finners; and we have all finned, and fallen fhort of the glory of God : we have done the things we ought not to have done, and left undone the things we ought to have done. And, fuch is the marvellous condefcenfion of him who inhabits eternity, that

he

he fent forth his Son, not with a meffage
of unrelenting vengeance, not to affign to
fallen fpirits a habitation in thofe realms
where the worm fhall never die, and the
fire fhall never be quenched, but with the
glorious and interefting meffage, that, whofoever forfakes his fins fhall be forgiven of
his Father who is in heaven, and whofoever frames his life and manners, in confequence of it, with this penitential affection, he fhall poffefs that inheritance which
is unfpeakably glorious ; his fins fhall be
cancelled from the book of the divine remembrance, and fhall not ftand againft
him in the judgement of the laft day. If
we confefs our fins, God is merciful and
juft to forgive us our fins. I diftinguifh
between the forgivenefs of fins and the converfion of our fouls. The forgivenefs of
fins is purely owing to the mediation and
the interceffion of Jefus Chrift; but the
work of converfion requires and calls upon
the object to be a co-worker with the influence of grace to purify the foul, and turn

its

its feet into the juft man's path, which is as the fhining light, that fhineth more and more unto the perfect day. Therefore, faith our Lord, *my Father worketh, and I work : work ye alfo.*

He came to his own, and his own received him not; but, to as many as received him, to them gave he power to become the fons of God, even to as many as believed on his name. Therefore, we experience the remiffion of fins through the forbearance of God ; but the work of fanctification is not yet completed ; the office of the Mediator is not only to procure for us the remiffion of fins paft, but it is to correct thofe vices in our very fouls which the gofpel-axe is laid to the root of, the corrupt tree in us, the root of our corrupt affections ; and, till this has effectually done its office, we fhall not be cleanfed from all unrighteoufnefs. God Almighty grant, of his infinite mercy, that we may not be content under any fpecious pretences of religion, but that we may feek to attain that

purity

purity of heart without which we cannot
enter the habitation of thofe glorious regions, where nothing that defiles, or that
worketh abomination, or maketh a lie, can
enter. It is the pure in heart who fhall fee
God : it is thofe that have been reformed
from the errors of their ways, and whofe
affections are raifed from earth to heaven,
from natural to fpiritual objects ; thefe
are of the number of the Lord's redeemed,
who, when the time of their conflict fhall
be ended on earth, fhall ftand upon Mount
Sion to celebrate the praifes of the great
King for ever and ever ! I feel my heart
enlarged with the love of the gofpel, with
the benevolent fpirit which ufhered the Saviour into the world : *Glory to God in the
higheft, on earth peace, and good-will to
men !*

We all ftand in the relation of brethren
to one another. We all ftand in the relation of children to the univerfal Parent.
We are his by creation. The Lord grant
we may be his by adoption : that we may

be

be fealed by him to the day of complete redemption : that we may be cleanfed from
all filthinefs of the flefh and fpirit : that
we may be influenced by the moft pure
motives to conduct ourfelves by his commandments here, and have a well-grounded
hope of living with him hereafter ! I
commend us to the protection of our Almighty Father ; and, finally, wifh us to
retain, in our remembrance, thefe important articles, that they may be written, as
with the point of a diamond, upon the tablet of our hearts. *He hath fhewed thee, O
man, what is good!* Confult the facred o-
racles : thou wilt be inftructed in that
which thou art to know, qualified to perform that which thou art to do, be enlarged in thy beft faculties and powers to enter
into thofe regions where the inhabitants
fhall not fay I am fick; for, the people who
dwell therein are forgiven their iniquity.

I commend you to God, and to the word
of his grace, which is able to build us up in
the moft holy faith, and to give us an inheritance

heritance among all them who are fan&i-
fied. *He hath fhewn unto thee, O man, what
is good, and what the Lord requires of thee ; to do
juftice, to love mercy, and to walk humbly with
thy God.* Add, to your faith, virtue ; to virtue,
knowledge ; to knowledge, temperance ; to
temperance, patience ; to patience, godlinefs ; to godlinefs, brotherly-kindnefs ;
and, to brotherly-kindnefs, charity : and,
if thefe things be in you, and abound a-
mong you, they fhall make you that you
fhall be neither barren, nor unfruitful, in
the faving knowledge of our Lord Jefus
Chrift !

DISCOURSE

DISCOURSE XI.

---

*I*T *is appointed unto men once to die.* This
is one of thofe propofitions which no
man is fo weak as to deny. But the facred
penman proceeds farther,—*and, after death,
cometh the judgement.* This, alfo, is a propofition which is of courfe admitted, in
terms, by every one who profeffes to be a
Chriftian, or a difciple of Chrift; and, indeed, this propofition is of the moft awful
and affecting nature. We muft all ftand
before the judgement-feat of Chrift, and receive a recompence of reward according as
our

our works have been. A Judge, who is infallible, who will not deceive, nor can poſſibly be deceived ; he taketh cognizance not only of our outward actions, but he penetrates the very thoughts and intents of all our hearts; and, ſeeing that he will not condemn the innocent, nor acquit the guilty,—on this reflection, methinks, it would be well for us, as it were, to lay our hands upon our hearts, and aſk ourſelves this queſtion, — What manner of creatures ought we to be ? The Author of our being is a God of infinite purity and holineſs ; nothing can be united unto him, no being admitted to dwell in his preſence, (in which there is fulneſs of joy,) who is in a ſtate of impurity : there nothing that worketh an abomination or that loveth and maketh a lie, can have an entrance : for, it is poſitively aſſerted by the higheſt authority, that, without holineſs, no man ſhall ſee the Lord. On the contrary, it is declared, *Bleſſed are the pure in heart, for they ſhall ſee God :*—that they ſhall have that

union

union and communion with him, in which the happiness of all ranks and classes of intelligent beings most certainly depends. But there is another proposition that it will be well for us also seriously to consider, *if any man say that he hath no sin*, or that he has not sinned, (as some have rendered this passage,) *he deceiveth himself, and the truth is not in him. We have all,* says the prophet, *as sheep gone astray,* — strayed from the paths of the just into the wilderness of this world. We have all sinned : we have all fallen short of the glory of God. In this state, therefore, whatever vain expectations any may entertain, they are not fit subjects of the kingdom of heaven : they are under the power and government of the prince of the power of the air, which ruleth in the hearts of the children of disobedience. Those, therefore, who are in this state, have no ground of hope of being admitted into the kingdom of the just; there is no communion between light and darkness, there is no fellowship between Christ and Belial;

R   and,

and, indeed, our Lord pofitively afferts, *If ye die in your fins, where I go ye fhall not not come* ; therefore, though he came (the meffenger from the Father was the Son of God, the eternal Word) with the glad tidings of the gofpel to all the inhabitants of the earth, yet his coming became, effectual only to thofe who received him. *I came,* fays he, *to my own, but my own received me not*; *but, to as many as received me, gave I power to become the Sons of God*; as much as to fay, Be ye not deceived, and imagine, that, in confequence of my coming, you are to be faved in your fins, or to have a licence from heaven to indulge your appetites. No: the purpofe of my coming is not to fave you in, but to fave you from, your fins ; and it is a faying that is worthy of all acceptation, *that Jefus Chrift came into the world to fave finners.* The Scriptures, propofe to us, and in a very explicit and comprehenfive manner, what we muft be before we can be accepted of his Father, who is in heaven. *Repent,* fays he, *and*

be

be converted, that your fins may be forgiven you : fo that it feems we muft, in the firft inftance, repent of thofe fins which we have committed. We muft really feel thofe penitential affections of foul that would prompt us, if poffible, to undo all the evil actions we have done; that would humble us moft effectually under a fenfe of our ingratitude to the Author of our being, and that would prompt us, in the depth of our humiliation, to fay, *a Saviour, or I die ; a Redeemer, or I perifh !* We muft not only repent of our fins paft, but we muft alfo be converted; not repent of thofe that are paft, and ftill purfue a courfe of iniquity, but we muft turn from unrighteoufnefs to righteoufnefs; our affections muft no longer be fet upon things that are upon the earth, but upon things that are above; we muft be no longer carnally, but fpiritually, minded; for, under the moft fpecious profeffion, to be carnally minded is death, but to be fpiritually minded is life and peace ; and, fuch is the infinite mercy and goodnefs of God,

through

through Jefus Chrift, towards us, that he wills not the death of finners, that is, to fee the eternal mifery, or infelicity, of a finner, but rather that all fhould return, fhould repent, and live a life of righteoufnefs here, and, of courfe, be glorified with him hereafter in the kingdom of the juft ; and the terms which he propofes are worthy of the Supreme Being to give, and would become us to accept with all penitence of foul and gratitude of heart. *If*, fays he, *ye confefs your fins, God is merciful* ; *he is juft to forgive us our fins* ;— not only to forgive the fins that are paft, but, by the operation of his grace, to fanctify us throughout, to forgive us our fins, and to cleanfe us from all unrighteoufnefs ; and, of courfe, if we become cleanfed from all unrighteoufnefs, we fhall be made meet for a habitation in the kingdom of heaven. Let us, therefore, be awakened to righteoufnefs ; awakened to righteoufnefs from the nature of the difpenfation we are under, that leads into every kind of purity and holinefs, that fo we may repent,

and

and alſo be converted, —converted at heart, and experience redemption through his blood, which was ſhed for the ſins of all mankind.

If we were thus . to contemplate the nature of the goſpel-diſpenſation, we, indeed, ſhould become circumſpeȼt, we ſhould be ſerious, 'we ſhould be inquiſitive ; and this prayer would become as it were habitual, *Create in me a clean heart, O God, and renew a right ſpirit within me* ; for, as it is the heart that is the objeȼt of converſion, by the power of an endleſs life, ſo it is the ſeat of ſin. It is there the prince of darkneſs has uſurped dominion ; and he, being caſt out, or the old man with his deeds put off, the peaceable kingdom of Immanuel is ſubſtituted ; that kingdom which cannot be removed. If this became the ſerious engagement of our hearts, we ſhould not only be induced to profeſs the Chriſtian faith, but alſo to exemplify the love of its Author, of our Father who is in heaven, by obſerving thoſe commandments which

R 3

are of univerfal obligation, and obedience to which is the rock which is immutable, a-gainft which the gates of hell fhall never prevail. It is not merely holding forth the truths of the gofpel that will render us acceptable ; thefe may be held forth in theory, and yet held in unrighteoufnefs, and will never avail us in the folemn feafon of the great day. Let us therefore advert to the clofe of that moft excellent fermon, preached upon the mount. After many practical doctrines concerning the kingdom of heaven had been opened to the hearers, our Lord took occafion to diftinguifh between the mere hearer of the word, the formal profeffor, and one that was a true difciple. *If any man hear my wcrds, and do them not, I will liken him unto a foolifh man who built his houfe upon the fand ; and the rains defcended, and the floods came, and the winds blew, and the houfe fell; and great was the fall thereof.* So will it be with the hope of the hypocrite, for it fhall perifh. The hope of the hypocrite may buoy him up

in

in the feafon of profperity; but, in the feafon of adverfity, it will fail him. When the rains fhall defcend, and the winds of adverfity blow, he will not be able to ftand the fhock. When he paffeth through the valley of the fhadow of death, this hope will be like the lamps of the foolifh virgins. *If any man hear thefe fayings of mine, and doeth them,*—(from which I infer they are practicable, and might be done, the contrary pofition implying the moft daring reflection on the attributes of the divine being :—does he command us to make brick without ftraw? command us to do that which we have no power to perform? far be it from the Father of mankind :)—*If any man hear thefe fayings of mine, and doeth them, I will liken him unto a wife man, who built his houfe upon a rock; and, when the rains defcended, and the floods came, and the winds blew, it fell not, becaufe* (not of any intrinfic merit of his own, but becaufe) *it was founded upon a rock,* the revelation of Jefus Chrift, the foundation of the apof-

R 4 tles

tles and prophets, Jesus Christ himself being the chief corner-stone, disallowed indeed of men, who would wish to build a
specious edifice on an unstable foundation,
who follow lying vanities in opposition
to every thing suited to an immortal spirit.

Let us, my friends, on this occasion,
(a solemn occasion it is to me; we have before us the remains of a friend, taken off
in the midst of her days, taken from the
society of the living; but nothing has hap-
pened to her that is uncommon :—in the
midst of life we are all in death, we have no
dependence on to-morrow,) let us, I say,
improve the present opportunity. Some,
indeed, fall off as fruit which drops when
it is come to full age, but others are, as it
were, cut off with a noxious blast by the
hand of him whose ways are all in wisdom.
It is ours, therefore, to submit ; and, seeing death is not assigned to any particular
age, (as the arrows thereof enter into the
habitations of the rich as well as the cot-
tage

tage of the poor; it separates the father from his children, the husband from his wife, the nearest and dearest connections in life;) let us, seeing we have no continuing city here, seek one above, whose foundations are laid in Zion, and are immutable as the throne of God.

I feel my heart enlarged, I trust, in the gospel of our Lord Jesus Christ, whose love constrains me to address you, my fellow-pilgrims, in this way. Let not the strong man glory in his strength, the rich man in his riches, nor the wise man in his wisdom; but, if any man glories, let him glory in this, that his Redeemer stands in the relation to him of one that is full of mercy and truth. *Let him glory in me, that I am the Lord, who exercise loving-kindness, judgement, and righteousness, in the earth :* let us be solicitous that we may be accepted of the Father of the human race, when we shall have done with these transitory things. Every thing around us will serve to instruct an attentive mind. It is

an

an awful truth, *Man that is born of a wo-man is of few days, and full of trouble: he co-meth up like a flower, and is cut down: like a shadow he fleeth, and continueth not.* With respect to many within the audience of my voice, the houses you possess were not long since possessed by your ancestors; they are gone; your children will soon have the same to say of you.

Let us therefore improve the present op-portunity, according to that measure of grace which we have received, that we may be sanctified in body, soul, and spirit; that we may have nothing to fear from that stroke which we cannot possibly shun; then, to us, to live will be Christ, and to die will be gain. Let us so conduct ourselves in this world, that, when the end of the world shall come upon us, (for, with res-pect to individuals, their dissolution is the end of the world with them,) we may not be surprised. Let us, before we go hence to be seen no more of men, endeavour to lay up a good foundation against the time

to

to come ; and then, when it fhall pleafe the great Difpofer of all things to fend the mef-- fage, whether in the early part of life, or in more advanced age, there will be hope in the death of the righteous. Their hope is full of immortality.

I commend thefe obfervations to you, and I commend you to God, and to the word of his grace, which is able to build you up, and give you an inheritance among all them who are fanctified by faith in the name of Jefus Chrift.

PRAYER

PRAYER

AT THE

CONCLUSION of the MEETING.

MOST gracious God, imprefs all our hearts at this feafon, we humbly befeech thee, with a fuitable folemnity to approach thy awful prefence ; that, infpired by the fpirit of grace, we may make an offering that fhall be acceptable with thee. We have, indeed, abundant caufe to acknowledge that we have not the leaft degree of merit to plead. Whatever any of us poffefs, that is good, is of thee, from
thee,

thee, and through the operation of thy grace. Be pleafed yet more and more to imprefs us in a manner fimilar to the poor publican ; that, under a fenfe of our own unworthinefs, we may call upon thy great and excellent name, with *Lord, be merciful to me a finner !* That, through effectual humiliation and penitence of foul, thou mayft be pleafed to cancel our tranfgreffions from the book of thy remembrance, be merciful to our unrighteoufnefs, and our iniquities remember no more : that, by the fanctifying influences of thy Spirit, our hearts may be alfo converted unto thee, that we may be cleanfed from all unrighteoufnefs, and enabled by thy grace to fteer our courfe, in future, in the juft man's path, which, as the bright and fhining light, fhineth more and more unto the perfect day : that we may pafs the time of our fojourning here in fear, and may conclude our fhort pilgrimage in thy favour, having a well-grounded hope that we fhall be accepted of thee, and admitted into the general affembly

bly of the juft, the Church of the firft-born, who are already triumphant in glory. O let us more and more feel the prevalence of the love of thy Son, and that it may be fhed abroad more and more in our hearts, and circulate more and more among one another : that we may put away all malice, and wrath, and love one another with a love unfeigned in Chrift : and O merciful Father, endue us more and more with that fpirit of charity that thinketh no evil, that is not eafily provoked, that extends not to our friends only, but alfo to our enemies, that we may lead one another to the beautiful mountain, the mountain of thy holinefs, where the lion and the lamb fhall lie down together, and a little child fhall lead them : that the kingdoms of the earth may become the kingdoms of the Lord and of thy Son : that thy name may be great, among all the tribes of the Gentiles, from the rifing of the fun to the fetting of the fame : that, O everlafting Father, thy creatures may be faved of thee with an everlafting falvation,

bring

bring thy fons and daughters from afar, to fit down in thy kingdom with Abraham, Ifaac, and Jacob, and praife and laud thy excellent name, who art worthy to receive the kingdom, power, and glory, both now and for evermore. Amen.

DISCOURSE

DISCOURSE XII.

OF a truth I perceive that God is no refpect-
er of perfons, but he that feareth him,
and worketh righteoufnefs, is accepted of him.
I prefume that moft of you are acquainted
with the particular caufe of this declaration,—that an eminent apoftle of our Lord
and Saviour Jefus Chrift feemed to have
been of the opinion, that the gofpel-mef-
fage was not to extend unto the Gentiles.
This was, perhaps, founded upon Jewifh
prejudice ; and we are inftructed, in this inftance, of the power of prejudice to ftop
the ears and blind the eyes of a wife man.

S   The

The moſt worthy and moſt exalted characters have, more or leſs, manifeſted in their
conduct the power of prejudice,—the prejudice of education ; and, indeed, the wrong
impreſſions, which mankind receive in their
minority, generally are laſting, or with
difficulty erafed. They ſeem to be like characters which are cut out upon a tree,
which grow wider and frequently deeper in
proportion to the growth of the tree.
Thus many prejudices, which mankind
have received at an early time of life, are
ſuch, that they have not been capable of
clearly diſtinguiſhing one object from another. They, as it were, grow with their
growth, and are ſtrengthened with their
ſtrength. I conceive theſe are thoſe ſecret
faults which the Pſalmiſt intended when he
faid, *who can underſtand his errors? Cleanſe
thou me from ſecret faults.* It ſeems that an
extraordinary difpenſation of divine providence effectually removed this prejudice
from the mind of the holy apoſtle. He
was · favoured with a viſion, in which he
saw,

faw, as it were, a fheet let down from heaven, containing various species of animals;
and he was commanded to arife, to flay, and
to eat; but he endeavoured to excufe himfelf by faying, that he had not eaten any
thing that is common or unclean; upon
which he was taught not to call that common or unclean which God had cleanfed.
The man to whom he was fent was a
man of a fincere heart; his heart was right
towards God; to him the glad tidings of
the gofpel were publifhed, though he was
a heathen. The mercy of God, through
Jefus Chrift, makes not that diftinction,
perfonal diftinction, between the human
fpecies which the law of Mofes made a-
mong the inferior animals, fome of which
were forbidden as unclean. The apoftle
faw the defign of this vifion, and there is no
doubt that he felt his heart enlarged in a
manner which, till then, he had been a
ftranger to. He now faw that the light of
the gofpel was freely to be preached to all
nations, kindreds, tongues, and people.

He

He faw that Immanuel was a light to enlighten the Gentiles as well as to be the
glory of the people of Ifrael. *I have fet
him to be a light to the Gentiles, to be for falvation unto the ends of the earth* ; not within
the narrow circle of any party of human
beings, not within the limits of any fpot
upon the face of the globe, but to be for
falvation to the very ends of the earth.
He, in the enlargement of his heart, breaks
forth in this manner, *Of a truth*, fays he, *I
perceive.* From which I infer that he
had feen, as it were, darkly through a glafs;
for, though, perhaps, friendly admonitions
may not effectually remove our prejudices,
yet, fometimes at leaft, they are conducive
to this end. We begin to fufpect we err,
and a man who begins to fufpect he errs is
in the way to underftand his errors ; whereas the obftinate may be compared to a man
who fhuts his eyes, and, of courfe, will not
be enabled to difcriminate objects even at
noon-day ; but the man, who begins to fufpect that he errs, or that he may err, begins

gins to open the door of his heart to conviction, and the apoftle feemed to have had
fome glimmering of this glorious truth;
but now the fcales of prejudice fell from
his eyes: his mental fight was clear. *Of
a truth, fays he, I perceive that God is no refpecter of perfons, but he that feareth God, and
worketh righteoufnefs, is accepted of him*;
and, I muft confefs, though it very unex-
pectedly appears to be my duty to confefs it
now, that, of all thofe doctrines which I
conceive to be errors, of all thofe things
which I conceive are not agreeable either to
reafon, to the nature of things, or to the
Scriptures of truth, there is not one which
to me is fo palpable as the doctrine of par-
tial election and reprobation; that is to
fay, that God, by virtue of his fovereignty,
did, of his own good will and pleafure, create a certain number of intelligent beings,
not only forefeeing that they would fin, and
be laftingly miferable, but for that very
purpofe; that their mifery is in confequence of his eternal decree; that the other

S 3   part,

part, whether few or more, are ordained to everlafting life ; not in confideration of any merit which they poffefs, (for, it is acknowledged that the elect poffefs no more merit than the reprobate ; that the righteoufnefs with which they are clothed is the righteoufnefs of Chrift ; that they are faved by virtue of the propitiatory facrifice of the Son of God ; that, by nature, they are black, they are vile, as the reprobate, but that they are comely with grace, as they ftand related to Chrift Jefus, who is the head of his Church ;) not in confideration therefore of any thing they can merit, but of God's fovereign pleafure. But I would wifh every one prefent ferioufly to confider, whether a greater reflection could be caft upon the divine attributes, unlefs it were to fay that he created all mankind to be eternally miferable. That God, the Father of the fpirits of all flefh, to whom we are indebted for our exiftence, and who of his pleafure did create us, fhould do it with a view of making us, or any part of his

creatures,

creatures, everlaftingly miferable, is fuch an idea that I confefs fhocks me. I fay it fhocks me. *Shall not the judge of all the earth do right ?* He is not only a God of juftice, but he is a God of goodnefs; but how can this be reconciled with goodnefs, that a Being fhould purpofely bring others into being in order to make them miferable? It is repugnant to every idea that I can form of the Deity. It is a difpofition, indeed, that appears to me to befpeak the nature of a tyrant, the nature of that being who is faid to go about like a roaring lion, feeking whom he may devour; but this, as well as other erroneous doctrines, is faid to be founded upon the Scriptures. Thus the Scriptures are made to contradict them-felves, the literal fenfe is adopted where that fenfe coincides with the pre-conceived opinion; but, where the literal fenfe ac-cords not with that opinion, it is tortured a thoufand ways to exprefs what the Holy Ghoft never intended, — whatever the par-ties wifh it to fpeak. Thus paffages, ob-

S 4   vioufly

vioufly figurative, have been confidered as literal; and others, appearing plain, even to common fenfe, to experience, to our common feelings, and to the nature of things, fuch have been rendered myfterious by various comments, in which truth has been obfcured by the multitude of words without knowledge. But, I conceive, if we confider the holy Scriptures, from the firft chapter of Genefis to the laft in Revelations; if we are capable of laying afide our prejudices; we fhall fee that they do affert the unity of God, his felf-fufficiency, his omnipotence, his omnifcience. The univerfality of his love to his creatures is the fcope and tendency of the facred pages, and *that* the motive of all the difpenfations of his providence to mankind. His views (if I may ufe that expreffion of the Ancient of days) terminated not upon himfelf, who is incapable of an acceffion of happinefs, neither upon the mifery of his creatures, to which he could have no motive, but they terminated in the creature who is capable

of

of immortality and eternal life. The Supreme Being, I conceive, to be the only perfectly diftinterefted being in the univerfe: perhaps, a parent, for inftance, (if the comparifon may at all be allowed,) a wife, an affectionate, parent, may bear fome humble refemblance of the univerfal Father. He is often fet forth to us under the endearing character of our Father : *as a father pitieth his children, fo the Lord pitieth them that fear him.* He knows our frame, he remembers that we are but duft ; but the parent, who poffeffes the moft delicate parental feelings, difcovers the utmoft folicitude for the happinefs of his offspring, and will find his happinefs intimately connected therewith. Such is the nature of that affection, ftrengthened by moral ties, that a parent and his offspring may be faid to be connected by fo many fibres of the heart : his happinefs is bound up in his offspring : he muft rejoice when they rejoice, and fuffer when they are afflicted. In alleviating their afflictions, he alleviates

his

his own : in promoting the happinefs of his children, he promotes his own felicity ; but, refpecting the divine Being, the analogy will not ftrictly hold. *Thy righteoufnefs*, as the text faith, *may profit the fon of man, and thy wickednefs may hurt a man as thou art*. The obfervance of the laws of virtue, of righteoufnefs, and truth, would promote the effential interefts of fociety. It would produce that harmony throughout all the claffes of focial life, in which the greateft degree of happinefs is to be experienced. Vice, on the contrary, is not only prejudicial to the interefts of the individual, but its evil influence extends, far and wide, within the circumference of fociety. Therefore, our righteoufnefs may profit men as we are, our wickednefs may hurt the children of men, but our righteoufnefs cannot profit him who is perfect, abfolutely perfect, abfolutely good, felf-fufficient, the fame yefterday, to day, and for ever, with whom there is no variablenefs, neither fhadow of turning. It is not the united

fup-

fupplications of all the fouls within the limits of his vaftly-extended empire that can
add to his effential glory, that can add to his felicity ; neither is it the neglect of the worfhip of all ranks and orders of intelligent
creatures that can diminifh his glory, that
can decreafe his felicity ; therefore, his motive, in creating and communicating good
to his creatures, muft be a motive perfectly difinterefted : it is love without the leaft
fpecies of alloy. God's love was the adorable motive of his making beings capable
of contemplating his attributes, and of that
felicity which is derived from him : this
was the glorious motive (if I may be indulged to fpeak of the divine Being by attri-
buting to him motives) that induced him to
create the various orders and claffes of intelligent beings, in this and every other
fphere, from the feraph above, that attends
upon the facred throne, to the loweft link
in the fcale of rational intelligent creatures.
And, in thus contemplating the Deity, I
find the beft affections of my heart excited
towards

towards him, my parent, in a fenfe infinitely fuperior to that natural relation which
fubfifts among the human fpecies and creatures : and, under this charaƈter, are we
inftruƈted to approach the Supreme Being,
*Our Father, which art in heaven, hallowed be
thy name*; in which there is fomething that
ftrikes me with peculiar force, that individuals, when they approach the facred altar
of the Lord Almighty, and prefer their pe-
titions to him who fees in fecret, are not to
confider themfelves as detached from fociety; they are not to implore the blefling
for themfelves alone. It is not *my* Father,
but *our* Father, which art in heaven, hallowed by thy name ; by which we are inftruƈted, that God is no refpeƈter of perfons, that we all ftand in the fame relation
to him, who is the God and Father of the
fpirits of all flefh. Remember that the
Scripture declares, that he is good to all.
Can he be good to them, whom, by an eternal irrevocable decree, he has configned to
everlafting mifery ? But God is good to
all ;

all; therefore he has not predeſtinated to everlaſting miſery the creature he has formed, which would be, in the moſt obvious ſenſe of the words, to be a reſpecter of perſons, and muſt ariſe from a motive of partiality. We are inſtructed to reſpect no man's perſon ; but this doctrine ſuppoſes that the divine Being reſpects perſons himſelf.

Various are thoſe paſſages of Scripture which might be educed, that bear a plain and obvious meaning, in oppoſition to this doctrine. And, though there may be ſome figurative paſſages of a doubtful tendency, in which the apoſtle aſſumes a borrowed ſtyle in his way of arguing with the Jews, yet I can never agree to explain plain paſſages by bold figures. We are abundantly inſtructed that he willeth not the death of a ſinner, but rather that he ſhould be turned, and live : that he ſhould repent, and be ſaved with an everlaſting ſalvation. We are alſo inſtructed, that, to them who ſeek for glory, honour, and immortality, God will

render

render eternal life; but, unto them who o-
bey not the truth, but obey unrighteoufnefs, *tribulation and anguifh, indignation
and wrath, upon every foul of man that doeth
evil, fo the Jew firft, and alfo of the Gentile*; for, there is no refpect of perfons with
God.

Let us, therefore, impreffed with what
I conceive are worthy notions of the Supreme Being, walk worthy of the vocation
wherewith we have been called. The power of the gofpel of Jefus is gone forth from
fea to fea, from the rivers to the ends
of the earth. The call of infinite mercy
and goodnefs is extended to people of all
names and all nations, to bring them into
a ftate of moral rectitude, to qualify them
for the fociety of the wife and worthy upon
earth, and for the everlafting communion
of the fpirits of the juft made perfect in
heaven: for this end is the gofpel preached
to every creature under heaven. I wifh
that it may be remembered with the folemnity with which it ought to be remembered,

bered, that it is not any fyftem of faith, it is not any profeffion of the purity of the gofpel of Jefus Chrift our Lord, it is not the acknowledgement of his miffion, it is not a fpeaking moft honourably of his a-dorable character, of his miniftry, of his crucifixion, of his refurrection, and afcen-fion into glory, nor of the propitiatory fa-crifice which he made for the whole world, that can render us acceptable to the Father of fpirits : the ground of our acceptance with God is upon the fame univerfal prin-ciple of righteoufnefs delivered by God in his remonftrance with Cain : *Why art thou wroth, and why is thy countenance fallen ? If thou doeft well, fhalt thou not be accepted ? and, if thou doeft not well, fin lieth at the door.* He was overcome by the power of, perhaps, one of the bafeft paffions the human heart is capable of. He was excited to deftroy his brother, becaufe the found that his offer-ing was accepted, that he had tokens of divine approbation. He was excited to flay him. The paffion of envy excited him

to

to fhed human blood on the earth. With this Cain, this murderer, the Author of the univerfe deigns to expoftulate in a very familiar manner : *Why is thy countenance fallen ? If thou doeft well, fhalt not thou be accepted ? but, if thou doeft not well, fin lieth at the door* : fo that, though, with refpect to external profeffion, and the external mode of offering their facrifices, they might be alike, yet, as the ftate of the heart of one was wicked, and productive of wicked actions, he was not accepted with his gift at the facred altar ; whereas, righteous Abel, who not only lifted up his hands to the habitation of God's holinefs, and conformed to the outward facrifice, but was juftly impreffed with a fenfe of his duty, became the object of the divine complacency : becaufe *thou haft loved righteoufnefs, and hated iniquity, therefore God, even thy God, hath anointed thee with the oil of gladnefs above thy fellows.* Though this, perhaps, may have a peculiar relation, as fome have confidered it, to the Meffiah, yet it feems alfo to have a relation

to

to a difcrimination among creatures,—*be-caufe thou haft loved righteoufnefs*; therefore,— it is not in confequence of a fpecious pro-feffion, not becaufe of an irrevocable de-cree,—but, *becaufe thou haft loved righteouf-nefs, and hated iniquity, therefore God, even thy God, hath anointed thee with the oil of gladnefs above thy fellows.* Oh! that there may be a proper emulation in us to excel in doing well. Ceafe, therefore, to do evil, learn to do well. As doing evil was the means of bringing down judgements upon the people of the Jews, fo they were in-ftructed how to avert the divine wrath, and render themfelves acceptable to the Father of the univerfe; not by an attendance to the rituals of that difpenfation,—*Bring no more vain oblations : incenfe is an abomina-tion unto me,* faith the Lord : *your new moons and your appointed feafts my foul hateth :*—but they were inftructed what to do : *Wafh ye, make you clean ; put away the evil of your do-ings from before mine eyes ; ceafe to do evil, learn to do well ; feek judgement ; relieve the*

T *oppreffed,*

*oppreffed, judge the fatherlefs, plead for the wi-
dow.* Here is a catalogue of excellent moral duties, here is an explanation of what
it is to do well. *He hath fhewed thee, O man,
what is good; and what doth the Lord require
of thee but to do juftly, and to love mercy, and
to walk humbly with thy God?* Now, fays he,
*come, and let us reafon together : though your
fins be as fcarlet, they fhall be as white as fnow :
though they be red like crimfon, they fhall be as
wool. If ye be willing and obedient, ye fhall
eat the good of the land.* Let us therefore
conform ourfelves to the terms by which we
are to be accepted. *Of a truth I perceive
that God is no refpecter of perfons; but, in e-
very nation, he that feareth him and worketh
righteoufnefs is accepted of him.* Let us
therefore cherifh in our breafts, in the firft
inftance, the emotions of filial fear, which
is diftinguifhed from that flavifh paffion of
which man is the object. Such a fear is
evidently to be diftinguifhed from that affection we have to the Ancient of days. I
compare that to the fear which an affectionate

ate child has of its parent, which fprings from love ; which, indeed, is the beft and moft worthy motive of our duties : we, therefore, fear not the Almighty Being merely becaufe he is armed with an uncontroulable power, and able to confign us to eternal woe, who rides upon a cherub, and the clouds are the duft of his feet, and doeth whatfoever he pleafeth :—we fear him not only becaufe of the attributes of power, but of goodnefs, the adorable attributes of goodnefs, mercy, and truth. He has dealt with us not in a way of rigid juftice, but according to the compaffion of a father. He has bowed the heavens, and manifefted himfelf among his creatures : for, he fo loved the world, that he fent his only begotten Son into the world, that whofoever believeth in him might not perifh, but have everlafting life ; therefore, let him be the object of our fear ; and of this fear many excellent things are fpoken as to its effects by way of prevention. It is a fountain of life to preferve from the fnare of

death :

death : the fear of the Lord keepeth the heart clean ; therefore, *bleſſed is the man that feareth always.* And, indeed, it is the firſt part of the everlaſting goſpel that was preached by an angel flying in the midſt of heaven, having the everlaſting goſpel to preach unto them that dwell on the earth, and to every nation, and kindred, and tongue, and people, ſaying, with a loud voice, *Fear God, and give glory to him ; for, the hour of his judgement is come ; and wor-ſhip him that made heaven, and earth, and the ſea, and the fountains of waters : fear ye him !* This principle of filial fear will incline our ears to an attention to his law, and we ſhall be meditators therein day and night ; and ſhall not only be hearers of the word, but doers of it. Under the influence of this fear, we ſhall work the work of righteouſneſs, the fruit of which is peace and aſſurance for e-ver.

If we obſerve this rule of right, if we conform ourſelves to him, we ſhall be uni-ted to the Author of our being in an union that

that is indiffoluble, and firm as the everlafting hills. *Keep my commandments,* (fays
Chrift to his difciples,) *and abide in my love;
even as I have kept my Father's commandments, and abide in his love.* Bleffed is the
man that keeps the commandments of God :
he fhall have accefs to the tree of life, and
enter through the gates into the city, become citizens with the faints, and of the
houfehold of God. God grant, of his infinite mercy and goodnefs, that, when the
days of our pilgrimage fhall be ended, we
may have an admiffion into the affembly
of juft and pure fpirits, to contemplate the
attributes of the *I AM :* that we may fing
the fong of Mofes, the fervant of God, and
the fong of the lamb, faying, *Great and marvellous are thy works, Lord God Almighty:
juft and true are thy ways, thou King of faints !*

PRAYER

P. R A Y E R

A T   T H E

CONCLUSION of the MEETING,

MOST gracious God, and Father of all, we befeech thee, manifeft thy presence, that, impreffed with the emotions of filial fear, we may approach thy holy altar with becoming reverence, pour forth our fouls unto thee, and offer thee a facrifice of thankfgiving and praife : that the contemplation of thy name may imprefs our hearts with peculiar folemnity. Thou, who ftandeft in the adorable relation to us of a father,

ther, thy goodnefs hath been extended to us from feafon to feafon, from the firft moment of our exiftence to the prefent moment. It is of thy bounty that we are fupplied with all thofe bleffings which we have received. Infpire us, we befeech thee, with the higheft fenfe of thy merciful goodnefs, that, O moft gracious Father, though heaven be thy throne, and the earth be thy footftool, continue, we befeech thee, to look down upon us with favour, and regard the low eftate of thy creatures. Sound an awakening alarm in the ears of the ignorant, thofe who are reclined upon the beds of eafe, who live in forgetfulnefs of thee, and of the obligations they are under to thee. O Grant that thefe may awake to righteoufnefs, that they fin not; that, under an awful fenfe of thy goodnefs, we may approach thy altar at this feafon, and offer to thee thankfgiving and praife, afcribing to thee glory, might, majefty, and dominion, and every other excellent attribute and

perfection,

perfection, of which thou art worthy, not only now, but alſo henceforth, and for e-vermore. Amen.

T H E   E N D.